IAN'S IONS AND EONS

Paul Levinson

Connected Editions

ISBN-13: 978-1-56178-052-5

Kindle: 978-1-56178-043-3

Cover design by: Joel Iskowitz

Printed in the United States of America

Connected Editions, 260 Underpass Road, #161, Brewster, MA 02631

https://connectededitions.com/

To Tina

PREFACE

This book contains the three "Ian" novelettes published thus far, at this point all in *Analog Science Fiction and Fact* magazine: "Ian's Ions and Eons" (April, 2011), "Ian, Isaac, and John" (November, 2011), and "Ian, George, and George" (December 2013). The stories are all written in the first person, by different narrators.

CONTENTS

IAN'S IONS AND EONS

That's what the neon sign said, in glowing script above the door. I don't know when it first opened. I had been out of town for about a year, and I never could get a straight answer out of Ian. I don't know what everyone else in the neighborhood thought, when they walked by Ian's on Johnson Avenue in the Bronx. Some kind of computer store, an electronic gimmick shop, a latter-day Radio Shack, perched on the second floor above a dry cleaner?

"We're a travel agency," Ian told me.

"Oh? Where do the 'ions' fit in, then?" I asked him. "Some kind of faster than hypersonic propulsion?"

"Nope. Not like that at all."

I looked around the store. It was nondescript. I guess that was a bit self-refuting. There was an old picture of the Parthenon on one wall, and a drawing of the Roman Colosseum on another, next to a stained photo of some Mayan ruin. "You specialize in travel to ancient places, like Rome and Athens, and that's where the 'eons' come in?"

"Something like that," Ian replied. He stroked his mustache. It was a fine mix of black and white. His hair was a little lighter, his eyes a little darker.

"What'll it cost me to travel back to 2000?"

"So you knew what we do, all along."

"Word gets around," I replied. "You'd be surprised -- or maybe you wouldn't."

Ian shook his head.

"So what's your pricing?" I asked again.

"2000 isn't too far back, we consider it part of the 21st century, a break for you. The rest of the price would depend on the purpose of your trip -- personal or societal?"

"Strictly personal."

Ian scowled.

***

He explained that nothing was strictly personal in his business -- you want to go back and kiss that girl again in the seventh grade, well that could still have unforeseen consequences for the world. And that meant such a trip required all the standard precautions, which were expensive. But they were less costly than protection from the possible results of a trip intended to change some kind of public event.

He quoted me a price, 20-percent less than the standard societal rate. "All inclusive."

"Jeez." I shook my head and whistled. "That's still a small fortune."

"You're welcome to try the competition," Ian said, blandly. He knew that I knew there was none.

"You'll need the complete payment up-front?"

"Obviously."

I nodded, and pressed in the desired dates of my journey on the thin terminal embedded in front of me on the counter. It fast-printed a 25-page itinerary. Ian still did some of his business the really old-fashioned way.

I looked at the first page. "A train?"

"Yep -- somewhere between Philadelphia and Wilmington. That's the way we do it."

"For the East Coast?"

"For any coast."

***

The itinerary was fairly explicit. Go down to Penn-Moynihan Station beneath the Farley Post Office. Fare already paid for, included in the package. Take the Tricela to Washington.

"Any Tricela?" I asked Ian. "They run every half hour, don't they?"

He nodded. "The specific Tricela doesn't matter. You supplied the date and time. It's the speed, the curve, and what they got going on down there, under the ground, between Philadelphia and Wilmington."

"That's where the 'ions' come in?"

He nodded, again. "Some kind of future underground technology produces them. They poke a little hole in the fabric of time. And if you hit it just right -- at the speed and angle at which the Tricela is traveling -- you get through."

"But it doesn't affect anyone else on the train?" I asked.

"It does not," Ian replied. "You have to be in just the right spot on the train, at just the right time. Plus, you need to be wearing this." Ian reached under the counter, rummaged around, and pulled out a blue-grey woolen vest with silvery buttons.

"You've got the 2000 model," Ian advised. "It's the micro-weave that attracts the ions."

I massaged the textile between my thumb and forefinger. "Feels like wool.... Ok if I try this on right here?"

"By all means," Ian said. "As I told you, the vest attracts the ions only on the Tricela, between Philadelphia and Wilmington--"

I tried on the vest.

"One size fits all," Ian said.

"Good," I said. "And how do I get this back to you?"

"It's all in the itinerary," Ian replied. He pulled the counter screen back towards him, and regarded it. "Let's see.... in 2000, you'll find yourself on a Metroliner. You do your business back there. Then get on a north-bound Metroliner. Wear the vest. And somewhere just south of Trenton you'll go to the right place in the train, and the next thing you'll know is you'll be back on the Tricela, heading north, in our time. The fabric of time 'remembers' you. It'll pull you back to the time you left, as long as you're wearing the vest. The fabric of time attracts the fabric of your vest. It's all in the itinerary," he said again.

I looked at it again. The relevant line began, 'Go to the Cafe Car, just as in the Tricela--' I nodded. "When exactly in 2000 do I arrive -- can I specify the arrival date?"

"You get there on whatever month, day, hour, minute, second you leave in our time. Nothing other than the year changes. Same with the return -- you get back here on whatever month, day, et cetera in 2000 you happen to find yourself on the Metroliner heading north, south of Trenton. It's all in the itin--"

"Okay. How come the jump to the past takes place between Philadelphia and Wilmington, and the jump back to the present between Philadelphia and Trenton?"

"Several reasons. The Metroliner has a space-time configuration slightly different from the Tricela - it's heavier than the Tricela, therefore cuts through space in a slightly different way - even when the two are moving at the exact same speed. And it's actually helpful that the going and returning happen in different places -- too much action in the same place could tear the temporal fabric with who knows what consequences." Ian shrugged. "That's what it is. The snap in the space-time continuum is 'elastic,' extending from Wilmington to Trenton. You all set?" His tone indicated he was about through with the conversation.

I tried one more question, anyway. "And you wouldn't happen to know who built this future underground technology?"

"I would not," Ian answered. "I'm just an agent selling tickets on a river boat. I have no idea how the river was created."

***

Many people consider the Post Office an anachronism. E-mail has been on mobile media for decades, and if you want to mail a package, hey, just fill out a Web form, and someone will be by your side to pick up your parcel in a under an hour, in most parts of the country.

One thing neither the Post Office or the Web could ever do, though, is mail people. That still required planes and trains. Fortunately, the famous inscription above the Post Office usually worked as well for trains: "Neither snow nor rain not heat nor gloom of night stays these couriers from the swift completion of their appointed rounds."

Trains had become swift. They usually kept their appointments. I knew it wasn't always that way. There was a time, right around the turn of the century, when most people thought trains were all but finished ....

I looked up at the inscription one more time for good luck, and hurried downstairs to board my Tricela. It was new and gleaming. I found my seat, reserved in the itinerary, and sat down next to a blonde. She was pretty nice, too.

"Going to Washington?" she asked, politely.

I entered my ID into the terminal on my arm-rest. It beeped confirmation. "Actually, Philadelphia." I didn't want her to wonder where I was when we headed south from Philadelphia.

She smiled. Her eyes were agate grey, and sparkled slightly in the soft train light. "Oh, I think you'll be going down to Washington, eventually."

I looked at her. "You're with Ian."

"Don't worry -- I'm included in the package."

"But you're not in the itinerary," I said.

"Ian didn't want you looking for me on the train - didn't want you to look as if you were looking for someone you couldn't find. That could attract attention you don't need. Especially given the significance of your mission."

The train sighed, and glided imperceptibly into its journey. My head felt as if it was moving a million times faster.

"So ... Ian knows I was lying, about my business being personal."

"Of course he does. How could he not? He checked the past and the future. It's his business."

She caught my expression. "Don't worry, I'm not here to stop you, I can assure you. I'm here to help. I'm part of the package," she repeated.

"But Ian charged me for the personal trip?" I asked.

The blonde smiled. "As Ian probably told you, there's really no such thing as a purely personal trip in time, as far as unforeseen major consequences go. We just keep the 'personal rate' as an incentive for our customers. People like a bargain. It's a lot of money."

***

The train sped under the Hudson. "Philadelphia, 20 minutes," an announcement advised. "Next stop, Philadelphia. No stops at Newark or Trenton on the Tricela."

"Think of me as your guide and your guardian," the blonde said. "My name's Ilene. With an 'I'."

"So Ian has no problem with what I really want to do in 2000?" I asked her.

"He has no problem with your plans for Washington. But people who listen in on Ian's Ions and Eons might feel differently. That's another reason he was happy to go along with your 'personal business' cover story."

I considered.

"Eavesdropping is unavoidable," Ilene continued. "It's cat and mouse, provisions to stop eavesdropping vs. eavesdropping, whatever the age."

"If I succeed, history could be hashed. Ian's ok with that?"

"He's mapped all of the time lines," Ilene replied. "He does well in all of them..."

"And me?" It couldn't hurt to ask.

Ilene arched an attractive eyebrow. "You know the terms and the rules. Ian makes no guarantees, except to do all in his power to get you to the past and back." She leaned closer. "And the guiding principle, always, is that once a plan is in motion, there are few certainties, positive or negative...."

***

The train slid out of Philadelphia. "Wilmington, next stop," the announcement said.

"Better get to the Cafe Car," Ilene advised. "You want to stand in the vestibule adjacent to the car. No problem if one or two other people are around -- the time disturbance will blind them for a split second. Then they'll have tears in their eyes. They'll think it's an allergy to the air in the train or whatever. When they wipe their tears away, they'll just think you moved on--"

7

"I know, it's in the itinerary."

She smiled again.

I looked at her lilac sweater. It was a thin weave, a snug fit. I doubted there was a vest or any other clothing underneath.

"Right," she said. "You'll be going alone. I'll be here for you on the Tricela back to New York."

"Looking forward to that."

***

I made my way to the designated vestibule. It was filled with passengers, overflowing from the line in the Cafe Car.

I tried to look as inconspicuous as possible.

To no avail.

"The guy behind the counter in there looks like he has arthritis," the man in front of me said. "The line hasn't moved in five minutes." He looked at me for confirmation.

I nodded.

The train lurched. Was this the launch of my jump through time? Seemed a minute or two earlier than the timetable.... I looked at my watch. It was exactly forty-two seconds too soon. And I was still in the same Tricela vestibule. It was just a lurch.

But it made the man even angrier. "Why can't they give smoother rides?" He clutched his stomach. "Maybe we're lucky we haven't eaten yet!"

I touched my own midsection in solidarity.

The man was not consoled. "I'm going back to my seat."
"Yeah." Actually, this could be a good tack -- let him think I went back to my seat, when the tears cleared from his eyes. I stroked my

vest.

But he was staring intently at me, a fellow traveler in suffering. No way he would not wonder what had happened to me ... when I disappeared just a second or two from now--

Ilene came through the door. She had on a nice short skirt on, too. She slipped and fell all over the man—

And I was off. Nothing lurched. It felt more like the cosmos had kissed me.

***

... after drinking some stinking beer. The place reeked of some kind of brew. I saw suds on the floor. The door opened. A woman with dark hair entered, and delicately side-stepped the wet part of the floor-- then swerved past me, as the train took another sharp turn. She steadied herself against the side of the vestibule.

It was definitely not the same compartment I had just been in. This one was bigger, warmer ... and stank of beer.

"Traveling to Washington?" she inquired, sweetly.

"And you would be?"

"Irene," she replied, and smiled.
"Everyone in Ian's organization has a name that begins with 'I'?"

"I know an Eileen whose name begins with an 'E'," Irene replied. "And we have an Ellen."

"Of course." Irene was dressed more casually than Ilene, in jeans and a plum-colored sweater. I didn't bother to ask her if some shade of purple was required for Ian's employees.

She gestured to the door. "I have a seat for you."

We left the vestibule and entered the adjacent car. The seats were plush blue.

"Don't let those cushions fool you," Irene advised. "This is definitely less comfortable than where you've just been. The past usually is."

I sat in a seat by the window, and she by my side. It was raining outside. Big beads of water pelted the pane, slightly stained with some kind of white. It had been crystal clear where I had just been -- the result of a sunny day and a new kind of genetically engineered glass. I hadn't realized it had been so clear, then, until now. Funny how you don't appreciate some things until you encounter their opposite....

Irene was right about the comfort. My back and legs were accustomed to better things. "So, anything special I should know about this time?" I asked. I realized I had not yet confirmed just when this was.

"The Supreme Court will announce its decision the day after tomorrow. Gore's people want the recount to proceed in Florida, Bush's do not. Everyone expects the decision to be very close. But you know that."

I nodded. Good. "Will you be ... helping me in Washington?"

"No," Irene answered. "I'm strictly for the trains."

***

We parted company in Union Station. "Remember, 1,000 bucks is the limit," she said, and walked away. She had given me a bank card for expenses. "Comes with the package."

I spotted an antique ATM and took out some cash. I broke a $10 bill for singles and change. I looked for a public phone. Good they still had them back here – mobile phones left trails.

The first five phones I encountered were broken, broken, in use, broken, in use. I got lucky with the sixth. I put in a quarter, waited for the tone, and carefully dialed the number I had stored on a piece of paper without a name in my pocket. I didn't want to fumble with the itinerary in public in the past. A man's voice answered.

I told him the reason for my call. It was dangerous, of course, but anything I did back here was dangerous and I could use his help and had no choice but to contact this guy. It was in bold letters on the itinerary.

There was a long silence. "Ok," he finally said, and gave me his address. Confirmation of what I already knew, but that was important.

I stepped outside into the rain and summoned a cab.

***

We sped through the slick wet streets of Georgetown, and pulled up to a brownstone on Wisconsin. The grey rain had given way to early evening.

I walked up the stairs. At closer view, the pits and scrapes were visible. The building had seen better days.

He was waiting for me inside the front door. He looked like his picture -- wire-rimmed glasses, straight brown hair combed back, button-down pin-striped shirt and an argyle sweater. Anonymous to this time and world, well known to me, even though I knew him only from his image. He looked to be about 25, but I had a feeling he was older. He looked me over, and nodded. I guess I looked enough like my picture.

He invited me into his ground floor apartment. It smelled faintly of butterscotch, not unpleasant.

We exchanged the usual introductions.

"What do I call you," he asked me.

"Tom, though it's not my name."

He nodded. "Eric, which actually is my name," he said.

"Right," I said.
"Good to meet you," he said, and we shook hands.
Then we talked.

"It's wrong," he said.

"The decision or—"

"Both," he said.

"Sometimes two wrongs can make a right."

He shook his head, dubiously.

"He'll be out of commission for only two months," I continued. "And if that cowboy gets into office—"

"I know the future as well as you," he said.

I nodded, but continued anyway, "we'll see the damaging effects far into the future."

"I know," he repeated, far less amicably, and he hadn't been too amicable the first time.

"So—"

"Their decision was wrong, outrageous," he said. "A coup-d'etat by the Court. It was wrong. They had no right to override the state on this. It went against their own principles. Most future historians agree. But removing the Chief Justice from the decision, making him unable to sit in this case—"

"His health is deteriorating anyway," I said. "This might well have happened even without my intervention."

"But it didn't." Eric looked at me. "So you're a subscriber to the principle of it's ok to make changes which accentuate or further what may already be happening on its own."

"Something like that, yes," I responded.

"And what if I'm in favor of not making any changes at all?"

"I'd wonder if what you are doing here is providing a fair consideration of what I propose to do, or if your mind is already made up on this," I replied. Eric came with the itinerary provided by Ian. He was supposed be one last check and balance, one less hurdle I had to overcome, in order to proceed. He was supposed to help with the logistics if my plan received his final approval. Except I had lied to Ian, and told him my mission was personal, and Ian had known that, I hadn't known that Ian had known that, so now I was here being grilled by Eric about my plan to incapacitate a Chief Justice of the Supreme Court. I guess that's what I got for lying.

"I can provide means to accomplish your mission, if I agree that it makes sense, and isn't too dangerous to the future," Eric said.

"Understood," I said. I knew I'd be entitled to a 50% refund if Eric said no, but that's not what I wanted. I also knew Ian's rationale for keeping his 50% if the mission was not approved -- "it's payment for the thrill of time travel, even if you're not given the final go ahead," the itinerary explained, and I couldn't completely

disagree. "So what do I do to convince you?"

Eric gestured to a chair. "Sit down and talk a little more about it. What are you drinking?"

***

I sipped a ginger ale. I envisioned my future, hypothetical biography, which of course would never be written, because time travelers inevitably had to be anonymous. "He was no fun when time traveling. Having a clear head trumped everything."

Eric apparently had no such mandates. He was on his second glass of dark red wine. He rested it on the maple coffee table, and turned to the paperwork he had prepared, and I had just gone through. I couldn't really begrudge Ian his 50% if my mission was not approved, if only because of this paperwork. It represented a huge amount of preparation and research, almost as much as I had done, and I had been working on this for years.

"So I think we can go quickly through the obvious basics," Eric said. "Obama will still be elected in 2008, even with Gore in the White House for the eight years before."

"Right," I agreed. "Lieberman won't get the nomination in 2008 -- he's way too centrist for the Democratic voters."

"A Republican in Democratic clothing, as his bio says," Eric said and nodded.
"And the immediate downsides of Gore as President?" I asked, though I knew it was really only one.

"His work on the greenhouse effect and his Nobel prize is postponed," Eric replied. "No big deal - the danger wasn't as imminent as they made it out to be back then, anyway."

I nodded. "And you might count as a downside that Gore in office won't stop September 11 -- but that's not really a downside to Gore, since it is highly unlikely that any President or administration could have stopped that."

"Agreed. Bush didn't. And Clinton was really no better at containing Bin Laden than was Bush. Hastings in the 2030s was not much better with Bin Laden's successor, and she had all kinds of early warnings going for her. They never see it until it's too late."

"Yep."

"Ok, let's look at the short-range positives of Gore as President," Eric said.

"No war in Iraq, no economic collapse worse than anything since the 1930s Great Depression," I said.

Eric agreed. "Those are impressive benefits, I'll grant you."

"And the economic is especially significant," I continued. "Without Bush mangling the economy, the U.S. continues as a superpower until well into the 21st century. Obama's able to build on the Gore prosperity, just as Gore built on Clinton. China grows, but doesn't dominate the world."

Eric agreed again.

"So where's the long-range downside?" I asked.

***

Eric took a long sip of wine before answering. "The space program could be damaged."

"The space program?" I asked. "Obama succeeding Bush made a big show of turning space exploration over to private enterprise, going to Mars not the Moon. Never really took off. And the space program continued to slide. Obama had no real choice, given the economic mess that Bush left him. Whatever money Obama had at his disposal was spent here on Earth. How could Obama succeeding Gore be any worse for space?"

"The focus on spending money to improve the Earth, before we extend to the cosmos," Eric replied, "really takes root in the Gore administration, according to our projections. Obama's not inclined to go against that. And since the Earth has so many problems, the Earth-first approach means we never really get beyond the planet, and space travel becomes a blip of the 20th century."

I considered. "A lot of speculation there."

"Yes," Eric said. "But that's what all of this is -- pro arguments as well as con to your intervention."

"The damage of the economic near-depression brought on by Bush is not speculation, it was very real, in our time line, and is still causing problems, including shrinking the space program, as you know."

"True," Eric conceded. "Perhaps Gore versus Bush is a draw in terms of our future in space."

"Agreed. Any other negatives?" I asked.

"Well, there is the immorality of nearly killing somebody," Eric replied.

"I want to prevent him from participating in the final decision, incapacitate him, not kill him," I replied.

"Without your intervention, Rehnquist dies of anaplastic thyroid cancer on 3 September 2005," Eric said. "He has less than five years of life remaining. It's an aggressive cancer. Obliging him to be hospitalized and sidelined from his life's work for even two months at this point is an action that should not be taken lightly."

I considered. "Fair enough."

Eric nodded. "Let's turn to the means."

***

I reached into my pocket and extracted a vial. "This will trigger all the symptoms of a stroke, which will continue on and off for about two months, but it won't be a stroke. There will be no lasting damage."

"May I?" Eric reached for the vial. I gave it to him. It was made of plastic as tough as steel, so there was no chance of it breaking. And I had two back-up vials in different parts of my clothing, in case Eric wanted to get nasty and lose this one.

Eric held it up to the light. "Good thing there are no customs inspectors at time travel portals," he said and smiled.

"That's more or less your job, isn't it, " I replied.

"True."

"When can I have your decision?" There was not much more for us to talk about.

"This is a very difficult matter," Eric replied.

"I know."

"Mixed potential consequences for society, plus always a problem when you diminish anyone's life."

I knew all of this, and saw no point in rehashing. Nonetheless — "You want to talk about this more? You need more time think about it? There are only two days until the Supreme Court's decision is announced."

He shook his head slowly. "You made your points clearly enough. No need for further conversation. I have just one final question for you, and then I'll give you my decision."

I looked at him.

"Why did you lie to Ian about the purpose of this trip being personal? It was more than the money. I need you to be truthful with me."

I saw no advantage in further deception at this point. "I was concerned that he might not have sold me this trip to 2000 Washington if he knew its real purpose."

"And yet here we are discussing precisely that purpose of this trip."

"Yes."

Eric sighed. "That's the way it is about time travel and truth. No matter how hard you try to disguise or avoid it, when you travel through time the truth sooner or later always jumps up through the floor board and bites you."

Ian was a businessman, this guy apparently was a philosopher.

"My answer is yes," Eric said.

I exhaled slowly. "I—"

"No need to be so relieved," Eric said. "It's in the itinerary. It says we make every effort to accommodate the time traveler's goal. And in difficult, close decisions, we side with the time traveler, not with conflicting historical situations or moral principles. It's part of Ian's commitment -- which also includes delivering the contents of this vial not to the personal relation you lied to Ian about, but to the Chief Justice of the Supreme Court of the United States."

I wondered why Eric didn't tack on some penalty payment for what must have been the far more difficult task of triggering a faux-stroke in the Chief Justice, but I decided not to press my luck with this conversation. For all I knew, Ian would be insisting on an additional hefty payment when I returned his vest. "How are you going to do that? You know someone close to the Chief Justice? A law clerk?" I had researched two excellent possible agents. For all I knew, Eric would be enlisting one or both of them. If not, or if Eric's special delivery failed to get to Rehnquist for any reason, I still had just enough time to use one of the vials I had in my pockets. But it made sense to let Eric do the heavy lifting. If his plan was to betray me, he could do that even if I walked out of here and told him I could take care of this myself.

Eric smiled. "You know I can't reveal those details."

***

I was hoping Eric might have offered a room to me in his brownstone - I would have liked to have kept an eye on him and the proceedings -- but no such luck, and it was not in the itinerary. I settled for a room in a comfortable hotel, and stayed focused on the television.

The news came through the next morning. Rehnquist was stricken, not clear as yet if he could continue on Bush v. Gore. I had researched this carefully. The case would be argued before the Court today, 11 December 2000. Had Rehnquist been stricken earlier, he might well have recovered and mustered enough strength to hear and decide this case. Getting the fast-acting pseudo-stroke inducer to him early in the morning was cutting it very close, and left little room for error, but there was no other way.

More good news on the television: Rehnquist would not be hearing the Bush v. Gore arguments today, and would not be participating in the decision. The court reporter on CNN explained that, in view of the importance of the case, the Court would have wanted to wait until Rehnquist was better and could sit with them for the decision. But given the urgency of rendering a decision in time for the electoral college meeting on 18 December -- the "safe harbor" for determining the electors having already been set as 12 December -- the Court had no choice but to go ahead with the proceedings without Rehnquist. I of course had no definite knowledge of how any of this would play out in the Court's decision in Bush v. Gore, only hopes and expectations. The good result wasn't part of the history I knew, the history I wanted to change. It was happening for the first time, due to my intervention, or, more precisely, Eric's getting the contents of the vial into Rehnquist. I watched with intense attention. I ate, drank, paced as I watched this primitive television. I kept half an eye on it as I went to the bathroom. The light from the two-dimensional screen hurt my eyes. But what I was seeing on the screen made me increasingly happy.

I slept fitfully with the television on. I showered and put on fresh clothes the next morning. After what seemed an eternity, but was only a matter of hours, the announcement was made: the Court had split 4-4 on the decision. Exactly the same as with the original 5-4 decision in favor of Bush, stopping the Florida recount, but with Rehnquist out if it. The split decision meant the Florida high court decision requiring the recount would be left standing. The recount would resume.

I ordered a celebratory meal from room service. The steak wasn't as good as in my time, too many antibiotics or whatever in this beef, but I enjoyed every bite of it anyway. Everything was falling into place. Bill Clinton addressed the nation in the evening. He thanked the Court for its wise decision, and wished the Chief Justice a speedy recovery. The Florida recount was complete and certified the next morning: Gore won the state by 1731 votes. I wanted to go out onto the streets of Washington and tell the world what I had done. I wanted to be hoisted on the shoulders of a grateful populace and cheered for my daring, trumpets blaring. But I knew better. Staying in the hotel room, interacting with as few people as possible, was part of the necessary regimen, written in big letters all over the itinerary.

Bush conceded the next morning -- 14 December 2000, a day after Gore had conceded in my history, because Bush had to wait for the recount. Gore made a gracious, healing-the-nation speech in the afternoon. I called Eric to thank him, but received no answer. I left no message.

I still had some money left. I ordered another good dinner, the best bottle of wine on the menu, and went to bed early. I had a train to catch, back to New York and my time, a better time than it had been, tomorrow morning.

***

I don't know what I had expected to see at Union Station the next morning, but it was great. Gore's victory headlined on every newspaper, broadcast on every radio, telling me this was real, real, real! I savored my eggs over easy and looked at the passersby. Truthfully, they seemed no happier than when I had arrived a few days earlier, when the results of the election were still in doubt. Maybe that was because half the country was Republican. I didn't really care. I had no idea whether these people would have seemed happier or sadder had the outcome gone the other way, with Bush the winner, before I had stepped in and made the change. All

I knew is that I was happier, because I knew what would have been. For that matter, if I understood how time travel worked, the only people who would know that there had once been a reality in which George W. Bush had been made the winner by the Supreme Court in 2000 would be me, Ian, and the people in Ian's organization. As a part of the reality that had changed this reality, we and we alone would retain knowledge of the original Bush-wins world, as I did right now.

I finished my eggs and coffee -- a little too acidic for my future taste buds -- and proceeded to the boarding gate. I patted my vest, for what must have been the 20th time, to make sure it was on. I would soon be back in New York. I knew there could be no guarantees about the consequences of changing the past, but—

"You seem very happy today, sir," the woman collecting the tickets at the gate said to me.

I broadened my smile. "Thank you. I am."

I walked to my train. Interestingly, the Acela -- direct pre-cursor, two models removed, from the Tricela in my time -- had commenced regular service on this line just a few days ago. It would have been fun to ride it, but the itinerary called for the older Metroliner, which would continue in service until 2006.

***

I sat in my reserved seat by the window, with an empty seat next to me in the aisle. I assumed Irene would soon be joining me, but recalled from the trip down that I wasn't supposed to look for any of the escorts Ian had provided for me. I half closed my eyes, put my head back, and saw a purple sweater and a smile. "Irene," I said and smiled back up at her.

She took the seat. "So it went well," she said.

I nodded.

"I bet you can't wait to see how your world's changed in the future," she said.

"That, and a decent cup of coffee," I replied.

"People who don't know any better think everything tasted better in the past," Irene said. "Not true. Depends on the time. The year 2000 is still a while before complete genetic engineering kicked in and the age of artificial ingredients washed out."

"Yeah." I'd been thinking of getting a cup of Amtrak coffee. Maybe not. But I was tired. I'd gotten at best one night's sleep in the past few days, on the night before I'd boarded the Tricela in New York City.

"We've got about two hours until your departure at Trenton," Irene said. "I won't take it personally if you take a nap."

I hesitated. "I don't know if I like the idea of falling sound asleep on a public train, in a time not my own. I don't know if that makes any sense—"

"It makes perfect sense," Irene said. "You're wise to be cautious. That's part of my job. To make sure no harm comes to you."

"And I do no harm to others."

She nodded.

I touched my vest, and closed my eyes, but didn't sleep. I daydreamed instead, about taking off that purple sweater, which was brushing softly against my arm. I switched from Irene to Ilene, from plum to lilac, and then to what I thought each looked like with nothing on at all. I led them to the bed in my hotel room. I thought I liked Ilene a little better. No, I liked them both. I was still in celebratory mood.

***

I took my leave of Irene a little south of Trenton, and walked to the Metroliner's cafe car. Irene had gone over the drill with me one more time. It was the same as on the trip down. I stepped in the vestibule at the back of the car, in the appointed place. This time the cafe was empty. The train clanked against the tracks, keeping pace with my pulse, and-

I got kissed again by the cosmos, a kiss far sweeter than even the ones in my daydreams. I opened my eyes, which had shut momentarily, involuntarily, and saw a leaner train. The ride was smoother, the contours around me more cleanly defined.

I looked down the corridor. A lilac sweater and sparkling eyes approached me. But I could see something more than sparkle in those eyes as Ilene got closer, and she was not smiling. For the first time in this trip I felt sick.

***

"How could that happen?" I had asked her this five times already.

"Please, don't shout," Ilene said, looking around the train car. "Attracting attention won't help any of us."

I shook my head. I had all I could do not to scream even louder. Fortunately, there were few people in this car, and most seemed asleep or entwined in their gossamer headphones. I didn't really care—

"Here, sit with me, let's talk," Ilene said, soothingly, and gestured to a seat by the window.

"You still haven't given me an answer," I said. I took the seat.

She sat down next to me. "That's because I really don't know. Please believe me."

There was a downy soft screen in front of each of us. I punched up Wikipedia on mine, and went to "George Walker Bush ... served as the 43rd President of the United States from 2001 to 2009 ...." I clenched my fist, and managed to punch just the cushion above the screen.

"I wouldn't lie to you about that," Ilene said. "I don't blame you for being furious."

"The recount had gone to Gore before I left," I said. "How did this happen?"

Ilene shook her head—

"How long have you known about it?"

"All of my life," she said. "The itinerary explains how that works. For me, George W. Bush was always President back then. Our history texts explain all about the recount, and how the Supreme Court stopped that—"

"And I stopped that Supreme Court!"

"I know," Ilene said. "I know. A part of me, a small part of me, remembers that you had indeed changed that. But—"

I looked at her. Her lilac sweater and agate-grey eyes were no longer so appealing. I started to stand. "Would you mind getting out of my way? You're no help to me here."

Ilene stood, but didn't move. "There's nothing you can do down in Wilmington. Trust me."

"I don't trust you," I said, with controlled raw anger. "But maybe I trust this process, a little. I know the weave in the vest was programmed to work only on the specified date. But maybe—"

"It won't work now," Ilene said.

Her deadpan tone was convincing. I didn't care—

"And if you leave now, I'll have to call the authorities. And if I don't put a call in to Ian soon, he'll call the authorities."

"A fine operation you run here," I said. "You take my money and— at very least, Ian owes me a complete refund and a big explanation."

"That's your only real option," Ilene said.

"Taking it up with Ian?"

She nodded.

"How do I know he'll even be there, in the Bronx?"

"I can call him right now," Ilene said. "And I can come with you to see him. Right after we get off of this train. I won't leave your sight."

That was as much to keep an eye on me, as my keeping an eye on her, I knew.

"You can take this up with Ian," Ilene said, again. "He'll know things about this that I do not."

***

It occurred to me, after I'd sat in edgy silence next to Ilene for at least 15 minutes, that maybe the screen in front of me had been programmed by her or Ian to give me the George Walker Bush bad news -- which wasn't in fact the truth -- for whatever twisted reasons Ian may have had.

"I'm going to the bathroom," I said and rose. "Is that all right with you?"

"I'll have to accompany you, at least to the door," Ilene said.

"Next stop, Newark," the train's voice announced.

We walked to bathroom at the front of the car. "Ok, I was lying," I told Ilene. "I want to see what Wikipedia says on another screen."

"No problem," Ilene said. She pointed to an empty seat and the computer screen in front of it.

"Let's walk forward a few cars," I said. "That ok with you?"

She nodded.

I picked an empty seat, suddenly, in the middle of the next car, and put up Wikipedia on the screen. I got the same infuriating words about George W. Bush.

Ilene looked at me. "There would nothing in it for Ian or me to lie to you about this now."

"I still haven't gotten over wondering what was in it for you and Ian to lie to me about this whole expensive trip in the first place," I said.

"I didn't lie to you," Ilene said.

I thought I saw, maybe, a tear in her eye.

"You want to check another screen?" she asked.

"I don't know," I said.

"If you saw the same on every screen, that still would not be absolute proof that George W. Bush was President and what you did was reversed," Ilene said, quietly. "For all you know, Ian could have gotten to every outlet on this train."

"I know," I said, tiredly. "For all I know, Ian could have hacked into every computer in New York City." The truth was that I didn't know what to think.

"He didn't," Ilene said. "Of that, I'm pretty sure. But that's why I think your only recourse is to talk directly to Ian -- he said he'll be waiting for us."

***

The MetroNorth spur left us about a block and a half from Ian's. We walked quickly to the glowing neon sign on the second story above the dry cleaner's on Johnson Avenue. Ian opened the door and invited us in.

"I don't usually do business so early," he said, without much of a smile. It was 2:20 in the afternoon.

I glared at him. "You—"

"You'd like me to explain what happened, I know," Ian said. "I can tell you that Eric did exactly as instructed. The pseudo-stroke inducer was administered. The Chief Justice was stricken and the Court decided the case without him, and the recount in Florida continued, making Gore the winner."

"I know that—" I said.

"He knows that—" Ilene said at the same time.

"You got exactly what was promised in the itinerary," Ian interrupted us both. "No less, no more."

"That's no answer," I said. I pounded my fist on the counter. I spoke quietly, but was even more furious than I was on the train. "I want to know how it came to be that Bush became President, even though, as you say, Gore was the winner."

Ian regarded me.

"I want to know, in other words, how it is that even though I got exactly what was promised in the itinerary, the state of reality now is precisely the opposite of what I was promised, as if what I was promised never came to be."

I could feel Ilene looking at me. I was 100% sure that if I made any kind of hostile move towards Ian, she'd be on me with who knows what kind of weapon. My fist on the counter had put her on the verge. This was no doubt also the reason that she had accompanied me here.

"You're not our only customer," Ian said.

"What?"

"You're not the only person who wants to travel to the past to right some wrong, real or imagined. You've got historical sympathies for the Democrats? There are just as many who feel the same way about the Republicans. Maybe more, since the Republicans are no longer around."

"And—"

"You're a smart guy. Figure it out. We're a business. Equal opportunity for our customers."

I thought for a moment and realized just what he was saying. "You're telling me—"

"That's right," Ian said. "I booked a trip for someone to go back and undo what you did."

I had all I could do not to wring Ian's throat and smash whatever weapon Ilene produced, smash it right out of her hand, and pummel Ian— But I controlled myself. "I swear to God I'm going to take you to court and sue you for every dollar you've got. You gave me a contract, the itinerary. You can't just—"

Now Ian smiled, slightly. "First of all, be my guest, take me to any court you like. No one will believe you. Even if they did, you'll find none has jurisdiction. Second, I didn't violate your itinerary in the slightest. You've read it. It has no non-compete clause."

"So," I was practically sputtering, "you sell trips to the past to people who want to change the past, and then turn around and sell trips to people who want to undo the changes? That's how you conduct this business?"

"Not all of this business, no," Ian replied.

"I'm not getting you," I said.

"Clause 37," Ilene spoke. "This is the first time I've seen it invoked like this."

"There is no 37," I said. I knew my damned itinerary by heart. It had only 36 clauses.

"Not in your itinerary, no," Ian said.

"There are other packages?"

"Yes, more expensive," Ian replied.

I was beginning to understand. "The societal itinerary?

"That's right," Ian said. "Our societal packages come with a Clause 37, which commits us to not selling a trip to any individual intent on undoing the societal change intended in the original itinerary."

"Why didn't you tell me that in the first place?"

"You lied to me. I asked you the purpose of your trip. You flat-out lied to me and said it was personal not societal. So I gave you the personal contract."
"You punished me for lying?"

"That's not the way we see it," Ian said. "You got personal enjoyment out of your trip -- you had the time of your life back there, just thinking that you had changed history, didn't you? That's what you paid for, and that's exactly what you received. No more, no less."

I also understood something else. "And you had no big problem with my lying, with my getting the contract without the Clause, didn't even charge me for the extra work Eric did with my target being a public figure like Rehnquist, because you knew you'd be able to sell a second trip to someone who wanted to undo what I did."
"I'm a businessman," Ian said.

"But I still care about the history ... Ok, exactly what would it cost me to go back a second time, and undo what was undone ... or ... but I guess the Clause 37 in the contract that succeeded mine wouldn't allow that."

"That's right," Ian said. "It's in effect a Clause that makes a trip to change something of societal importance in the past a one-time only event, or a part of history that we allow to be changed only once. It's the only way we can maintain some modicum of sanity in these circumstances. Otherwise, we'd be losing our minds with history changing back and forth, back and forth, ad infinitum. As you know, we here at Ian's maintain memories of all the histories —"

"I know." My mind was speeding through possibilities. "But maybe I could still purchase another trip, one which would have nothing directly to do with the 2000 election. But one which would still have the same ultimate effect. Like if I did something to make George Bush the father lose the 1988 election for President, or—"

"But I couldn't sell you a trip like that, if you told me that was its ultimate purpose." And now Ian was smiling, almost fully, for the first time.

"I understand," I said.

"And a trip like that would be very expensive," Ian said. "Societal, and earlier than the 21st century. Could you afford it?"

"I'm not sure."

"I know one way of reducing the cost," Ilene said, looking tentatively at Ian.

Ian nodded, slightly. "Your middle name is Isidor, is it not?" he asked me.

"Yes, but I never use it."

"Think about using it," Ian said. "We give a 50% discount to employees."

IAN, ISAAC, AND JOHN

I approached Ian's Ions and Eons at the end of a bitterly cold winter's day. I liked the way the setting sun played off Ian's neon sign. It was warmer, of course, inside the store. I knew it would be a lot warmer in the time I wanted to go.

Ian emerged, with the same scowl and mustache he'd had on his face the last time I'd seen him, which was several months ago. "You took your time," he said, with a slight smile.

I guess that passed for humor from Ian. "I'm still not completely pleased with the itinerary," I said.

Ian shrugged.

"We're in New York City right now," I said. "I want to travel back to New York City, January 1975. Surely there's an easier way than taking a train down to Wilmington to make the jump, and then getting back on a northbound train to New York City."

Ian almost laughed, derisively. "There's nothing even remotely easy about time travel. That's probably the first thing you need to learn."

I didn't like being lectured. I started to say so, and realized I'd probably do better here keeping my mouth shut. Besides, I had no other choice.

"You're welcome to try the competition," Ian said, anyway, "though I gather you've looked into that, and you're back here now because you know there is none."

I nodded.

Ian eyed his screen. "The preliminary itinerary I worked up for you still looks viable. Your purpose is still a mix of societal business and personal pleasure?"

I nodded again. "That's right."

"Well, we appreciate your honesty -- I'll give you that," Ian said. "You know that we'll need to charge you the straight, higher societal price -- no discount even though part of your agenda is personal."

"Yeah, you explained that clearly last time." This was what was really bothering me about the deal, not the inconvenience of taking a train south from New York City to get to New York City. But I didn't like being the cheapskate. Now that I was talking to him, it occurred to me that Ian probably realized that, too.

"And the fee for a trip back to 1975 is steep -- no digital products in hand back then, which means much more prep for us to do."

"I'm good for the money."

"We'll need it all upfront," Ian said.

"That's what I meant," I replied.

"So you're ready to sign?" Ian asked, and swiveled the screen around to me.

I nodded, tried not to think about the price, and signed the screen.

***

The timing was just right -- I'd planned it that way. Ian had all the arrangements in place within two weeks of my signing the itinerary. I boarded the Tricela in New York City three days later.

I proceeded to my assigned seat, next to a woman with long ringlets of blond hair, soft gray eyes, and wide lips that certainly curved nicely when she smiled at me. I was barely in my seat when she spoke to me. "Lannie Jones?"

I finished confirming my seat on the console in front of me. "The itinerary says no one outside of Ian's organization was to know of this. I assume you're with Ian?"

She nodded. "Is Lannie Jones your real name? A lot of our clients use aliases -- we don't mind. Ian knows who you really are, anyway."

"Part of his making sure there are no ulterior motives for the trip?" I asked.

"Yes."

"Believe it or not, Jones is not an alias, neither is Lannie," I said. "And you would be?"

"Ingrid," she said. "We in Ian's go on a strictly first name basis."

The train sped into the tunnel under the Hudson, and announced the next stop: Philadelphia.

"I'm here to make sure this part of your trip runs as smoothly as this train," Ingrid said. "You all set with the steps in the itinerary?"

"Yeah." I touched my vest. Hard to believe that this weave was essential to my trip to the past and back, but, then again, time travel was hard to believe, and it wasn't my field in any case. The closest I got to string theory was a suspended 5th on my guitar. "Actually, I'm still not completely comfortable about what's supposed to happen in the Cafe Car. I'll just disappear at the precise time, but what do I do if there are people hanging around? I have no control over that."

"You just take care of being in the vestibule next to the Cafe Car at the right time, and try not to attract anyone's attention," Ingrid said. "Just stand quietly in a corner. If anyone gets too friendly, it will be my job to distract them." She smiled. "But don't look for me, because that could get people near you to look at you."

I looked at her lips. I bet she could be distracting, at that.

***

I left Ingrid as the Tricela glided out of Philadelphia. The Cafe Car was empty - no customers in need of Ingrid's distraction there or in the adjoining vestibule. But the bearded man behind the counter spotted me across the car and through the entrance way -- I was unfortunately right in his line of sight -- and I realized that if I just stood there he might well see me disappear. He had no one else to look at. I opened my phone. Three minutes to go. Would Ingrid come in and engage him in conversation? No point in just passively waiting for that-

"Colombian, jet black, please." I ordered the coffee as I quickly approached and put the cash on the counter.   It was already brewed and ready to serve, but he still moved as if he was 110 years old.   I took the coffee and thanked him. He was saying something about the cold snap but I barely heard.

I couldn't have had more than a minute left. I walked to the trash receptacle -- it was not in the counter-man's line of vision. With any luck he wouldn't be looking in my direction anyway -- I was no longer a potential customer. I risked a quick sip of the coffee -- Tricela's was justifiably renowned as delicious -- and threw the rest with the cup in the trash. I looked at my phone. Forty-three seconds to go.   Too bad, I could have had another sip or two.   I savored the fading taste of the coffee, walked into the vestibule, closed my eyes, and—

Whoosh. Something else touched my lips. That's what it felt like. The heavier train beneath my feet and its shake, rattle 'n' rollin' against the track confirmed it. I was in a different place than I'd been a second ago. I hoped it was 1975.

***

I walked through a couple of cars just to take it in. Unless I'd been whisked into some kind of period movie about the 1970s, the people on the train said the same as its weight and shake. Their accents were a little odd. Like they were deliberately speaking with New York and Philadelphia intonations. I guess language had become more homogenized in my time. And they looked just as I'd expected, just as I'd seen in numerous pix and clips, too. Same cuts of hair, same loud colors, same just-post-psychedelic feel. I smiled. It was a good time.

I looked at my itinerary, which I had printed out on paper, consistent with no portable or even personal computers in 1975. It called for me to get off the train in Wilmington, and catch a Metroliner back up to New York. I felt my pocket for the ticket, and walked to the end of the car and the exit. The conductor announced that the train was arriving in Wilmington. A gent in a black shirt and a redhead in her twenties joined me at the exit. The train pulled into the elevated station, stopped, and swung back and forth to a full halt. The door opened and we exited.

"I'll be going up to New York with you," the redhead said, and pointed across the tracks. "My name is Evelyn." I looked at her more closely. Keen blue eyes, pastel flowery shirt, and nice tight blue jeans. "Good to meet you, Evelyn," I said, but she looked to me like sweet Suite Judy Blue Eyes. "You're with Ian?"

She nodded at me and then at the stairs. "The northbound Metroliner is due here in 16 minutes. It'll take us at least 5 minutes to walk down the stairs, across the station, and then up the stairs on the other side. We don't want to run and attract attention."

I walked with her. "Ian likes cutting it close."

"Too much time between connections creates possibilities for unexplained mishaps," Evelyn said.

I let her walk a little ahead of me. The jeans fit differently in this era, too. Better than in mine. Maybe that's why they sang about them in the music -- no, that was at least a decade earlier. But they still looked good. I caught up with Evelyn. "It's balmy down here," I said.

"Sixty-eight degrees Fahrenheit," she said. "And not just here, and not because we're south of New York. It's close to that temperature there as well."

We walked quickly down the stairs. I touched my vest. "It was less than a third of that temperature when I left New York," I told her. "Good thing this vest has some new wool woven into it."

Evelyn looked like something about that didn't make sense to her.

"It's a gen-engineered fabric, accentuates the properties of natural wool, warm in winter and cool in summer," I said.

"I know," she said, and stopped near a locker on the side of the station. I gave her the contents of my pockets, including my phone, but not my ticket. I took off my vest, and handed it to her, all as called for in the itinerary.

She put all of the items into a small bag that she took out of the locker. "No, I was thinking it's a good thing it's not cold up in New York right now, otherwise we would have needed to get you something warm to wear ... I'll hold on to this until you to take the return train down from New York."

"Yeah, thanks." The itinerary called for me to store the items with whomever asked me for them down here, to prevent their accidental discovery in 1975, which was far enough back in time that their showing up could have serious, unpredictable ramifications.

We walked up the stairs and across the platform to the northbound train. We looked down the track. No train was yet in view. Evelyn gave me a wallet with money and ID.

"You have $500 in cash there," she said. "And a nice ID. We figured we couldn't go wrong keeping your same last name."

We both chuckled and looked south again for the train.

***

The train back to New York was musty, stuffy, hot but not enough to make me sweat. Reminded me of the gig I did in Rio last year. I said goodbye to Evelyn in Penn Station. "I'll be here for you on the train back to Philadelphia tonight," she told me.

I nodded and left the train. That next trip would be down to Philadelphia, then turn around back up to New York, for the return to my time right before Trenton. A convoluted route but, considering where it took me, no standards applied.

The air in Penn Station was sickening, almost unbreathable. I made my way by stairs and escalators as quickly as I could to the outside. Sunshine and a speck of soot on my cheek welcomed me to New York City, January 1975. This was an age before clean air laws had fully kicked in, but the air outside was much better than in the station. I hailed a cab. "West 4th Street and 6th Avenue," I told the cabbie, whose face had the map of Ireland written all over it.

The ride uptown felt like a stagecoach, or what I imagined that to be. It made the train seem smooth as silk in recollection, but I loved every minute of the jostling, groaning springs, and the blaring horns and sounds of swerves outside. The clothing and pace of the people on the streets were even better than on the train.

"Keep the change." I gave the cabbie a ten-dollar bill, five times the fare but hey the fine ride was more than worth it. The Village was more of the bright historical tapestry, plus roasted peanut aromas and hotdogs on carts and music everywhere. The January heat wave had brought out the singers and the guitarists. I half expected to see Dylan singing "Shelter from the Storm" on the corner, but I doubted Dylan was doing street corner singing in 1975 anymore, if he ever did.

"Like a sun that starts to rise, in the cream of morning skies ...," a guy with a straggly mustache was singing to his friend, like he was teaching him the song. I didn't recognize it but I liked it. I looked for a tip jar or an open guitar case, but the guy was singing a capella. I smiled at him and he smiled back.

I was half-tempted to go straight up to Electric Lady Land, but I supposed I'd better make the call. I saw a phone booth on the corner. A guitarist was leaning against the wall, halfway between me and the phone. I had no trouble recognizing what he was singing, as I walked by. Yeah, no trouble at all, and it broke my heart. John Lennon's "I'm Only Sleeping." I put a ten-dollar bill in his guitar case.

"Thank you, man!" he said, and resumed the song.

I'd spent $20 out of $500 in just the past few minutes, but it didn't matter. I wouldn't be here too long. I walked quickly to the phone booth -- I couldn't listen any longer to what the guitarist was singing.

I pulled the itinerary out of my pocket, put a dime into the phone, and waited for the dial tone. It came pretty quickly. I dialed the number.

"Hello," a man voice's answered.

"I'm Lannie Jones," I said.

"You can come right over, Mr. Jones," he said. "I'm Isaac." He gave his address. "A brownstone, 2nd floor, off Washington Square Park. I'll be waiting for you downstairs."

***

Isaac looked to be in his late 20s. He had on a pull-over shirt and jeans. "Mr. Jones?"

I nodded. "Lannie's fine."

He extended his hand. I shook it.

"Come on up."

We walked up a pinewood flight of stairs. Isaac ushered me into a big, one-room apartment. He sat at a table in the middle of the room. "Have a seat," he said. "Oh," he said, after I took a chair. "Anything to drink? Coffee, tea, soda?"

"You still have Seven Up back here, right?" I asked.

"Yes, we do," Isaac said, as he opened his refrigerator, "but not in here.... How about Sprite?"

"Never heard of it."

"It's lemon and lime, like Seven Up," Isaac said.

"Ok."

He brought me a fizzing glass. It tasted good.

He picked up a thin folder from the table. He opened it. "This is pretty straightforward -- the easiest I've seen in a while."

"Good," I said.

"Let's just go over it, so I can assure Ian I did my job," he said.

"Sure."

"So ... you're a direct descendant, that's why this is personal as well as societal."

"That's right," I said.

"And you're going to improve one of the mixes on the Young Americans album that David Bowie is making at Electric Lady Land?"

"That's it," I replied.

"David Bowie's real name was David Robert Jones," he said.

I nodded.

"He's going to get a pretty big hit off the album -- 'Fame' -- but you'd like to see it do even better. Because you think that with that big a record, back now, Bowie's name would be that much bigger in your time, and that would help your career."

"Yep."

"Makes sense," Isaac said, and nodded, more to himself than to me. "And you can take of the mechanics. I have an additional ID for you here, as well as keys. No one is expected to be in the studio between 6 and 8 pm tonight. And should someone find you fooling around with the tapes, you have the ID as an additional producer Bowie brought into this."

I nodded.

"Excellent," Isaac said. "These sorts of changes have little impact on society as a whole, and raise no pressing ethical questions."

I nodded again.

"Excellent," Isaac said again.

"Good." I looked at the clock on the wall.

"Just one thing," Isaac said.

"Yes?"

"I'm not sure if I believe you."

***

I sipped my Sprite then pushed it away. "I bet this is just a poor performance of Seven Up."

Isaac said nothing.

"I don't appreciate being called a liar," I said.

"Then convince me that you're not," Isaac replied.

"I don't even know what you think I'm lying about."

"Don't play games with me," Isaac said. "You're a musician, you're an expert on the music of this era. You know exactly what I am talking about."

"Enlighten me."

"Your attitude right now is making me even more suspicious," Isaac said. "Bear in mind that if I don't give you the key, you'll have no access to the Electric Lady."

"But you're claiming I may be lying about that, anyway," I said. "So why should that faze me?"

Isaac exhaled in irritation. "Ok, you want me to spell this out to you? Here it is: There's no way, given your immersion in the music of this time and place, that you don't know that John Lennon was on some of those Electric Lady sessions with your ancestor, David Bowie."

"You think I came back here to warn John Lennon?"

"The thought occurred to me, yes," Isaac said. "Are you going insult my intelligence and tell me it hasn't occurred to you?"

"Of course it has," I said. "But why I would come back here to 1975 if I wanted to warn Lennon? Wouldn't I have been better off booking a trip to 1980, maybe just a day or two before that bastard shot him in front of the Dakota?"

Isaac nodded. "Better off -- yes -- but not if you were afraid that Ian wouldn't have approved your trip, and you would have been right."

"So you think I had in mind warning Lennon all along, and I just blatantly lied to Ian?"

"I'll let you in on a little secret," Isaac said. "Just about all of Ian's customers lie to him, one way or the other. It's inevitable in this business."

"I'd say it's inevitable in life," I said. "But didn't you just tell me that no one's supposed to be in the studio between 6 and 8 tonight? I assume that no one includes Lennon?"

"It does," Isaac said. "But he's in the city. For all I know, you researched where he is, or found his phone number, and you're planning on contacting him before you leave."

"What can I do to convince you that I won't do that -- that I'm here just to improve David Bowie's standing in musical history?"

"Actually, there's nothing you can do," Isaac said.

"Then why the hell did Ian approve my mission in the first place?"

"Think of Ian's Ions and Eons as a bank," Isaac said. "Ian owns the bank, and also acts as the loan officer. I'm the underwriter. I work for Ian, but he relies on me and the people who do this job to give the final authorization."

I thought about jumping this damn "underwriter" and taking the keys. I hadn't been in a fight since I'd punched Sheldon Tzuna in our junior high school yard over a girl in the seventh grade, but Isaac looked like he'd never thrown a punch in his life.

"There's a simple solution to this," Isaac said.

"Tell me."

"The pleasure clause in your Itinerary says that we won't breathe down your neck once you leave this apartment, that we understand that being on your own is part of the fun of this trip back, but I'm prepared to authorize an alteration, if that's ok with you."

"And that alteration would be?"

"You stay here with me until 6 pm, I accompany you to Electric Lady, and then back on the train to Wilmington, back up to New York, until you make the jump back to your future time near Trenton. I'm sure Evelyn will have no problem with that."

I looked at the clock on Isaac's wall. It was already 10 past 5. "I guess I have no problem with that either." I clearly had no choice.

***

Electric Lady Studios at 52 West 8th Street was a little off 6th Avenue, and less than a five-minute walk from Isaac's brownstone. It was 6:07pm when we reached the studios, and well into darkness, which was a little disconcerting, since the high temperatures felt like we were in late spring or early summer.

"This sits on an underground tributary," Isaac observed, as he opened the front door with his key.

I wasn't in the mood for small talk. We walked up to the second floor. There wasn't a soul around, just as we'd expected -- except maybe the ghost of Jimi Hendrix, who'd financed the construction. The studio was wide open and ready for my ministrations.
First task was getting the multi-track tape for "Fame" and the already mixed-down version. According to my research, they were in a room in the back of the studio -- which was locked. But Isaac had a key for that. I located the tapes and cued them up in the mixing board in the studio. I'd worked on virtual versions of this mixing board for months back in my time.

"Fame" was 4 minutes and 22 seconds -- that would be the album cut. The single would be shorter. But what I intended to do would work for both. Pretty simple, really. Bring up the bass, mix it a little more closely with the drum, and make sure Lennon's voice was more recognizable in the mix. I now had about 90 minutes -- if we needed to be out of here before 8pm -- to do the job. I'd do as many practice mixes as I had time for, and then record my better mix over the current mix already on the output tape. The changes I would make would be subtle but profound. I doubted any of the engineers here in the studio would notice. But I was betting the public would respond to the better mix.

I started doing the new mixes. I noticed that Isaac, to his credit, was grooving to the music almost as much as I was. Give him that.

I was finally satisfied at 17 minutes to 8 pm. I recorded my mix over the one already there, and returned both tapes -- the multi-track and the new mix tape I'd made -- back to the proper place in the room where I'd found them.

"You did good work," Isaac said. I didn't know him well enough to know if he meant it.

"Thank you," I said.

We walked down the stairs and out the door. "We can catch a taxi uptown on 6th Avenue," Isaac said. I could feel his eyes on me as we walked.

We passed a guy with long hair, a long thin nose, and horned rimmed glasses. He was frowning. Isaac frowned even more after we'd walked past him. "Robert Christgau. That dyspeptic professor gave your Young Americans album a B-."

"Never heard of him," I said.

"No loss," Isaac said. "Music critic for the Village Voice -- he's panned everyone from Paul McCartney to Phil Ochs."

I turned around to get a better look at him, but Christgau's back was barely visible.

Isaac hailed a cab on 6th Avenue.

***

Isaac stuck closer to me than white on rice, as I'm pretty sure some Southern song from the early days of rock 'n' roll had it. We entered the southbound Metroliner. I had a ticket, Isaac bought his with cash when the conductor came around. The train eased out of the station and under the Hudson.

Evelyn approached us near Newark. Her keen blue eyes were none too happy when she saw Isaac. "What's going on?" she asked, and took an adjacent seat.

"A necessary adjustment," Isaac said, smoothly. "My call."

"But breaking protocol," Evelyn said. "You have your job, I have mine, and mine's the train." She looked at me, not pleased about having this conversation right in front of me, but what else could she do.

"I'll file a full report explaining why I needed to do this, when Mr. Jones' trip is over," Isaac offered. "I would have filed it already if I had email access back here." Isaac smiled.

Evelyn did not, and continued looking at me. "I'm impressed," she said to me. "I had you pegged as a straightforward, above-board traveler .... I guess there's no such entity in this line of work."

"You didn't talk to Mr. Jones about his interest in music on the trip up here?" Isaac asked. "John Lennon never came up?"

"That's what this is about?" Evelyn asked in return.

"That's what it's almost always about, when someone with a life's passion for music comes back to New York City, 1971-1980," Isaac replied.

"It was a grossly senseless, horrendous assassination," Evelyn said, and shuddered. "I can't really fault anyone who would want to change that."
"But your job is to stop anyone who wants to change that history, unless Ian approved it—"

"Which we both know he never would," Evelyn interrupted.

"You enjoying this?" Isaac suddenly turned on me. I was sure nothing on my face expressed enjoyment.

"We shouldn't be talking in front of him—" Evelyn began.

"Doesn't matter," now Isaac interrupted. "He won't get a chance to do anything more back here than get on that northbound train to the future near Trenton."

"Do you know what his plan was?" Evelyn asked. Then to me, "sorry, I don't mean to talk about you as if you weren't here." Then to Isaac, "is there evidence that he intended to derail that awful killing?"

"I saw Mr. Jones' face when Lennon's name came up in conversation," Isaac replied. These people had more interest than my girlfriend in my face.

"I came back to improve the mix on that 'Fame' recording," I said, "and I did that. But tell me: what would be the problem if someone did save Lennon? Why is that so anathema to you? It's not as if he was a President or even an important politician or anything."

Isaac smiled sadly and shook his head. "The eternal question. In some ways, saving Lennon could be even worse, with more unpredictable consequences. I'll bet you more people loved Lennon and the Beatles, more people were affected by them, then even JFK -- who, had he lived, would only have been President for eight years, and would have likely in that period of time antagonized a lot of his original supporters."

"I don't know if I agree with that," Evelyn said. "And the protocols say political changes are the ones we have to give the most extensive consideration."

"I'm going to the bathroom," I said. "Is that consistent with your protocols?"

"Sure," Isaac said, "as long as I come along with you." Then to Evelyn, "see, it's good that I came along. I can make sure he doesn't leave a message on the bathroom mirror."

***

The conversation continued like that -- mostly Isaac and Evelyn talking about John Lennon, talking about me, sniping at each other -- all the way to Philadelphia. I was never left alone. Evelyn got coffees for the three of us, then Isaac did the same. It was nearing 10pm when we approached Philadelphia, and everyone was tired.

"30th Street Station next stop," the conductor announced, "30th Street Station, Philadelphia. Please check for your belongings before you leave the train."

I realized that Evelyn had not yet given me the contents of her bag -- most importantly, my vest. I looked over to her. She was dozing. No, she wasn't dozing, she was sleeping, pretty soundly. I could sympathize, everyone was exhausted, but it seemed a little odd. And something about the way her body was slumped back in the seat, her mouth open, eyes open a little too, bottoms of her blue eyes glinting in the light which was still on above her—

"I drugged her," Isaac said. "Not to worry."

"What?"

"You heard the feeling she has for Lennon and his music," Isaac said. "I couldn't let her head back to Trenton with us -- I can't keep an eye on both of you at the same time, if she needs to use the ladies' room—"

"You're really obsessed with Lennon, aren't you?"

"Whatever it takes," Isaac replied.

The train was pulling into the 30th Street Station.

"I need my vest -- it's in her bag," I said.

Isaac nodded and moved across the aisle. He looked in the overhead compartment -- nothing was there. He moved Evelyn as gently as he could to the empty seat next to her, and didn't seem to mind getting his hands on her body. Her head lolled against the window. Isaac looked under the seat in front of her. "Ah!" He produced the bag.

He beckoned me to stand. "Let's go."

"You're just going to leave her here?"

"She's in good company." Isaac gestured to the rest of the train car. At least half the passengers were sleeping. "She'll be out until Washington, and I'll call ahead to have a few of our security people meet her there."

The train came to a slow stop. I took a last look at Evelyn, tufts of red hair now covering most of her face, and left the train with Isaac.

***

We had a 15-minute wait for the northbound train in the 30th Street Philadelphia station. The train would depart in 1975, and before it reached Trenton, I would be in a northbound Tricela in the future, back in my own time. I looked at the big, classic clock on the wall. Fifteen minutes could be a long time.

I put on my vest, and turned on my phone to make sure it was still working.

"You won't get any service here," Isaac said, with a big grin. He seemed almost manic. "Don't look so grim," he continued. "Even if you had managed to talk to Lennon, it's unlikely it would have had any effect. He doesn't know you. You would tell him, what, stay away from the Dakota on the evening of December 8, 1980 -- get the hell out of New York City altogether? Why would he believe you? You didn't bring any evidence with you from the future, and even if you had, Lennon would have doubted it, tagged you as nutcase. The most likely result would have been only John telling Yoko hey I got a call from someone daft."

"I could have told him about his Double Fantasy album to establish credibility. Won't come out until 1980," I said.

The station master announced that our train would soon be arriving.

"Yep, we don't have much time," Isaac said. "Come with me." He walked with me to a phone booth. "Please stand right here. If you run, our security will find you. I'm calling them right now about Evelyn." He entered the phone booth, and pulled the doors shut around him. I assumed he didn't want me to hear what he was saying to security -- whether about me or Evelyn -- but I had pretty good ears. I heard him put coins in the phone. He was speaking softly, but I got some of what he was saying ...

"John Lennon ... Lannie Jones ... may sound crazy ... stay away ... Dakota ... man who understands strange things ... that's right ... December ... just like starting over ... watching the wheels ... yeah ... just remember ... please ..."

Isaac hung up the phone and walked out of the phone booth.

The station master announced that our train was now arriving.

"Let's go." Isaac took me by the arm and down the stairs to the arriving northbound train.

"What were you telling your security people?" I asked. "I heard a little and it didn't make much sense."

Isaac started to reply, but was distracted by two large men, approaching us quickly from the southern part of the platform. Two other men of the same stature approached us from the northern side.

The train came into the station. Its doors opened.

The four men were upon Isaac. "What—"

Evelyn came down the stairs. She was completely awake. She didn't look the least bit rested.

"We need to get on this train," she told me. I looked at Isaac. The four men were escorting him back up the stairs.

"Now," Evelyn said.

She and I got on the northbound train.

***

"Trenton's not that far ahead," Evelyn said. "We might as well stand."

The train started pulling out of the station.

I looked at her. "You were out cold on that southbound train."

She smiled, slightly. "I was a theater major at Fordham. I know how to act. I knew better than to drink anything Isaac gave me."

I looked back at the platform, to see if any other unexpected escorts had shown. Nothing but a few slow-moving passengers still walking to the stairs.

"So the security that Isaac called for you came to get him instead?"

Evelyn hesitated before answering. "Isaac didn't call our security," she finally said.

I thought about what I had overheard. Isaac had mentioned my name, and John Lennon's, but the conversation didn't sound like something anyone would be having with security. Not that I was an expert about any of this—

"He was leaving a message on John Lennon's answering machine."

"He—"

"Isaac was trying to warn Lennon," Evelyn said.

Yes, something about what I'd heard rang true about that. What had Isaac said ... "watching the wheels"? Wasn't that the name of a song on Double Fantasy? Yes! And so was "starting over" ... Son of a bitch -- Isaac was using knowledge of those songs to establish his creds with Lennon, demonstrate to Lennon that Isaac had knowledge of the future, just as Isaac and I had discussed before he made the call. Lennon would indeed likely dismiss the call now as the act of crank, but when he started writing those songs, he'd remember .... Maybe Isaac's saying those words would even encourage Lennon to write those songs. My head was spinning watching the wheels of paradox ...

"But why did Isaac say my name to Lennon? What purpose did that serve?" I asked.

"He wanted Lennon to think that you, not Isaac, was leaving the message. That way, if Ian found out about that, he would hold you not Isaac responsible."

The conductor announced that Trenton was the next stop.

"We better get to the Cafe Car," Evelyn said.

"You're coming with me?"

"In this case, yes," Evelyn replied. "Not to the future, but to the Cafe Car. Given what has happened, we can't take any more chances."

***

My mind was still spinning. I knew I had just minutes or less left in 1975. I had Lennon's phone number, too -- stored in my head, like a lyric. But the phone I had in my pocket was useless here. I hadn't been sure before this trip if I would contact Lennon. I still wasn't sure. But what Evelyn said Isaac had done, what I had half overheard, inspired me.

We reached the Cafe Car. "You'll need to step inside," Evelyn said.

"Did Isaac succeed?" I asked.

"No way of knowing that back here, right now," she replied. "You'll know as soon as you get back, and check the Wiki on the Tricela."

There was an Amtrak phone, in a luxurious booth, right next to the Cafe Car.

"Don't do that," Evelyn commanded, "don't even think about it. You'll miss the jump point, and Ian will charge you seven times what you already paid, the penalty for setting things straight. Bold letters in the itinerary."

I figured I had seconds left.

It couldn't hurt for Lennon to get a message from another daft nutjob. I made a move for the phone booth—

And reached the arm of another big security man. I flailed and punched. But he lifted me in the air with one arm, opened the door of the Cafe with another, and tossed me in.

I hit the floor hard, got up on one leg, and felt the lips of the cosmos on mine once more. The last thing I saw in 1975 were Evelyn's lips, not smiling.

***

I got to my feet on a smooth Tricela. Ingrid was standing right next to me, smiling.

"I'm back in the future," I told her. "Lennon's long dead, either in 1980 or whenever after. You still need to keep such a careful eye on me?"

"Most returnees are glad to see me," Ingrid replied, still smiling. "I hear you had an eventful trip back there."

We walked out of the Cafe Car. "What -- they gave you an instant briefing on me?"

"Think about it," Ingrid replied. "Anything that happens in the past is in principle instantly knowable in the future, especially if the people in the past want it that way."

We reached our seats. Ingrid directed me to take the one by the window.

"So how did I do?" I asked. The itinerary said everyone involved in the time travel at Ian's remembered the before and after.

"Fame became a #1 record, just as you'd hoped. Bowie's first record to make #1 on the Billboard charts. His career and his legacy are considerably better than when you left. He now ranked #29 in the 2002 BBC poll of the 100 Greatest Britons, and #39 on Rolling Stone's 2004 100 Greatest Rock Artists of All Time. But he never quite became a household name in his lifetime, if that's what you wanted. Fame, apropos the song, is complicated. It's based on so many factors -- changing just one thing, even if it's crucial, is unlikely to change everything. But you did very well with this. You can read it all for yourself." She gestured to the screen sewn into the back of the seat front of me.

"And Lennon?" For some reason, I had trouble getting those words out of my mouth.

"More complicated still."

***

I grabbed a coffee from the robocart. "Tell me about it."

Ingrid took a tea. "Isaac's message in 1975, warning Lennon, got through to his answering machine, as they called it back then, as far as we know. "But Lennon was shot to death on December 8, 1980 by Mark David Chapman at the Dakota anyway."

"So Lennon either never heard Isaac's message, or he quickly discarded it. Somehow Lennon carefully listening and then just forgetting about it seems unlikely," I said.

"That's what we think, too," Ingrid said.

"So ... something, someone got in the way of Lennon hearing that message? And that would be who, Ian, wouldn't it?"

Ingrid shook her head no. "Not the way Ian works. We do our utmost to prevent any changes that go beyond the ones outlined in the itinerary. But if something unauthorized does get through, Ian learned a long time ago not to pursue it any further. We're not time cops, we're private enterprise, and we don't officially police the timeline. And if we ran around trying to correct any unauthorized changes, we could do a lot more damage than the changes themselves."

I didn't know if I bought that, especially given the impassioned arguments I'd heard back in 1975 about the severe unpredictability and danger of altering the history that killed Lennon. "Well, if not Ian, who then?"

"Ian would like to talk to you about that -- if you're amenable -- when you return the vest."

***

Our train slid into Penn-Moynihan in New York. It was nearly midnight, but Ingrid assured me that Ian's would be open, and the man in charge would be very happy to see me. She accompanied me to the Metro North Riverdale spur, which brought us to a block and a half away from Ian's at 12:15am.

Ian's neon sign did look especially cool against the cold black sky, with no moon to rival the sign's liquid light. Ian opened the door with his customary scowl. "Mr. Jones," he said.

Ingrid and Ian exchanged nods, and Ingrid left with a smile that included me.

I nodded at Ian, and returned the vest, as called for in the itinerary.

"I hear you had a little bit of an outburst back there, at the end, Mr. Jones."

"I—"

"But no harm was done, so I've decided to give you a complete refund." He swiveled his console around, so I could see the exorbitant amount I had paid for this trip completely returned to my account.

"But—"

"Yes?"

"I accomplished what I wanted on my trip," I said. "I got to remix 'Fame,' and it indeed became a #1 record and helped my ancestor's career."

"That's right," Ian said.

"So why the refund? Not that I mind it—"

Now Ian smiled a little. "You also helped us accomplish something we here at Ian's have wanted to do for quite some time –– root out an unstable member of our organization."

"You mean Isaac?"

"That's right," Ian said again. "We've known for quite some time that he was determined to use his trusted position with us to stop John Lennon's assassination. He jumped at the opportunity to be your 'underwriter,' as he liked to put it. He played you perfectly, and he was confident that he'd could tip off Lennon, but make it look as if the tipster were you. Fortunately, we played him even more perfectly than he was playing you, and Evelyn was right there to catch him in the act."

"But not before he left the message for Lennon," I said.

"Right again."

"So what got in the way of Lennon actually hearing that message, or reacting to it?"

"Most likely, you," Ian replied.

"You're out of your mind!"

Now Ian smiled a little more. "Think about it. You've gone back to the past, shuffled the deck -- or the musical mix, in this case -- so you're the descendant of a pop icon much brighter than when you left. As the months and the years go by, you'll begin to enjoy that, as you should. But a part of you will always worry about how you made that happen, and whether someone else could make something else happen that could eclipse your ancestor, eclipse what you worked so hard to achieve. You'll become the greatest defender of the historical status quo -- of the history just as you made it. And that will include Lennon's assassination in 1980."

I shook my head vehemently. "No."

"As I said, give it time," Ian said. "But look, we can do a little test of what you truly want right now. You think you would do almost anything to stop Lennon's killing -- you regret that you didn't do more when you were back in 1975. I think one reason you didn't was you were already beginning to have an attachment, even back then, to the history you made, exactly as it was. But here's a proposal: I just refunded all of your payment, as you saw. I'd be happy to use that, and only that, as a complete payment for another trip you could make to the past. It could be a trip to kill Mark David Chapman. That would be the best way to 100% assure Lennon's survival. Ordinarily, those kinds of missions are far more expensive than even what you paid. But it's yours for free, right now. What do you say?"

"I don't know if I'm a killer," I replied.

"Fair enough," Ian said. "But there may be other ways you can stop Chapman, without killing him. Should I work up some possible itineraries for you? You choose, all free."

"I -- I need to think about it," I said.

"Understood," Ian said. "That's just what I thought you'd say. But think about it, think about all of this. My offer holds for any trip you want to make to that past -- including making sure that Lennon does not hear or react to Isaac's message. I'm giving you the full range of options."

It was clear from Ian's tone that our discussion was over for now.

***

I walked out into the dark, frigid Riverdale streets. I turned around for another look at Ian's Ions and Eons, and my phone beeped. A message had come in, while I'd been talking to Ian. A big promoter, from Madison Spiral Garden, wanted me to be part of a band that would be playing at a 20th century rock retrospective. All the musicians would be descendants of stars from that era. "You belong there, as David Bowie's descendant," the message concluded.

I had a feeling I'd be liking my life a lot better now. Ian was probably right that I wouldn't want to do anything, wouldn't want anything to happen in the past, that might change my new life. But ... would I really go back to the past to make sure Lennon didn't get Isaac's message, to insure Lennon was at that foul pit entrance to the Dakota in 1980? That's what Ian was tempting me to do, hoping I would do. And I— No, no! I was not that kind of human being! Not that selfish! How could I let Lennon die, when his music had brought me such pleasure? He deserved to live his life, whatever the consequences to my professional success and vanity —

I clutched my phone, walked a few more steps, and turned around. I started walking, half running back to Ian's. I bounded up the stairs and pounded on the door. I had no idea if he was still inside -- I hadn't seen him leave -- for all I knew, Ian slept here.

He opened the door, again with the scowl.

"I'd like to book that trip to the past, to 1975, for as soon as you can get this all in motion."

Ian raised an eyebrow. "That was fast. And the purpose?"

I thought for a second. Ian was much more likely to approve my trip if I told him it was to make sure, somehow, that Lennon didn't get, or do anything in response to, Isaac's message. In fact, I doubted if he would approve the trip, in spite of what he had said, if I told him my true, sure purpose now -- just the opposite -- which was to make sure Lennon heeded Isaac's brave warning. But would Ian believe me, if I lied? Would he find a way with his devious mind to make me serve his not my goals if he sent me back there?

"Your purpose?" Ian asked a second time.

There was no outsmarting this guy, I knew that. I had control over my actions, not how Ian manipulated their consequences. I would say whatever it took to get Ian to approve another trip, and then do what my soul wanted once I was back there again. If my efforts to save Lennon didn't work, if they somehow propelled Lennon not to take seriously but laugh at Isaac's message, well ... only history knew the outcome.

IAN, GEORGE, AND GEORGE

I an walked towards his little shop on Johnson Avenue in the Bronx, looked up at the glowing neon sign that proclaimed its name, and scowled. He had programmed the neon to flicker, just a little, last week. To give it a touch of mid-20th century authenticity, a time that was especially appealing to him because it was just beyond the range of his agency. But now that he looked at the cool neon script, flickering in a pattern designed to look random, he was concerned that customers might not get the historical detail, and mistake the effect for a faulty sign. That was unacceptable -- the last thing Ian wanted to do was introduce any uncertainty into the minds of customers who were paying him a lot of money for a trip to the past and back. An unstable sign, after all, could also be a sign of an unstable system that provided shoddy access to a vent in the space-time continuum.

I looked at Ian shaking his head on the screen in my hand from my vantage point around the corner. I smiled. If I knew Ian, he was thinking about whom could he blame for this blunder in self-proclamation. And I knew Ian a bit about now. I'd made it my business to know everything I could about this consummate businessman, including installation of a variety of micro-cameras to record his moves near and in his store, which I was reasonably sure he didn't know about. It was the least I could do, given that I was about to put a lot of money -- not to mention my life -- in his hands, once again.

Ian entered the building. I gave him a few minutes to get up to his "Ian's, Ions, and Eons" on the second floor, and I walked over to conduct our business.

***

He was still scowling when I entered his office -- presumably not about the sign, because it was no longer flickering when I reached the storefront. He looked up from behind the counter and nodded.

"All set?" I asked.

"I have your money and your signature," Ian replied, "all that I need." He looked at my papyrus-weave jacket. "I wouldn't wear that tomorrow -- you'll be traveling into a brutal heat wave. Mid-90s Fahrenheit."

"Ok."

Ian reached under the counter and came up with a dark paisley vest. He rubbed the fabric between his fingers, as if he was fathoming the texture, and gave the garment to me. "I put nasal suppositories in the right pocket. You may need them, given the heat where you're headed, and the consequent smell."

"Thank you," I said. "But I like to savor everything in the places I visit, including the aromas."

"Suit yourself."

"I only wish there was some way I could go back a few decades further," I said. Not really, I was just saying that to gauge his reaction.

Ian's scowl deepened. "You know the limitations."

"I guess I'm thinking that limits are only absolute to the extent that someone has yet to figure out how to break through them."

Now Ian smiled, with scarcely more joy than conveyed in his scowl. "I don't care what you do or try to do about those limitations, as long as you're back on that northbound Metroliner on July 28, 1970."

***

It certainly wasn't too hot the next morning, as I walked up to Moynihan Station, gleaming in the sunlight on 33rd Street and 8th Avenue.   In fact it was beautiful, and the air was sweet with the locust and hibiscus trees planted up and down the streets and along the new overpass, too.   I breathed in slowly and sighed. A parting, living postcard, to wish me well and encourage my return.

I sauntered down the stairs.   Plenty of time to catch the train.   I bought a cool lemon-cantaloupe juice -- my favorite for this early in the morning -- and looked around.   I wondered if I could spot Ian's train agent. There was a 66.66% chance her name started with "I," and a 33.33% chance it started with "E," but I didn't see nametags shimmering on anyone.

I leaned against a pillar and contemplated the holographic display on the far wall. Half a dozen Tricelas were approaching Moynihan from north and south, dicing up the light as they plied their ways through the morning.   They were the closest emissaries of Biden North American InterRail, which glistened in the background on the screen like a great circulatory system made of phosphor. These would be the last three-dimensional images I'd be seeing for a while.   Where I was going, it would all be two-dimensional, and inside rather than outside the screens.

***

I found my reserved seat on the train and tried to get comfortable. She soon took the seat next to me, in a snug, thin lavender outfit of linen.

"Iris," she said, and extended a hand.

I took it and started to tell her mine—

"No need for pleasantries," she said. "As you know, I'm just going to brief you here -- briefly brief you," she smiled at her own wordplay, "and leave before the train pulls out."

"Right," I said. No pleasantries, but I couldn't help notice that she was aptly named, with rich earthy brown irises that warmed your soul.

"You've utilized Ian's twice before, with good results, so you know how this works -- you make your move between Philadelphia and Wilmington."

"Yes," I said.

"This trip is a little more ambitious, but the fundamentals are the same. Ok ... any questions?"

"What happens if someone sees me in the Cafe Car, just as I'm—"

She waved a dismissive hand.   "Not the problem that amateurs imagine it to be -- as you know, because you're no amateur."

"I know," I said, "but I have still have concerns."

She waved her hand again. "Your disappearing would be chalked up as hallucination, if anyone happens to see it. You were wise to take the no-accompaniment option -- you shaved some bucks off a very expensive trip, given that 1970 is so close to the terminus." She stood and smiled again. "I better get out of here before the train starts."

I watched her walk away down the aisle. I was known here as a generous patron of the arts, but sometimes I was too cheap for my own good. I wouldn't have minded Iris' company on the swift trip to Philadelphia.

***

The Cafe Car was crowded, which was probably, ironically, the best way to do this. Someone suddenly vanishing was a lot more likely to be noticed when one of a few, not a bustling many. I looked at my wristwatch, which I had already donned. One minute 18 seconds until the cosmos touched my shoulder and spun me like a top back to 1970, at the same exact time and day of the month as now. I stroked my paisley vest with my thumb. I hoped Ian had gotten the nano-weave right, which would pull me into the speed and angle and place of this train in the space-time fabric at the right moment and leave me in the same place on a very different train, a Metroliner, headed to Wilmington, Delaware in 1970. For some reason, I always worried about that weave the most, but it had worked as advertised twice before -- actually, four times, traveling and returning, safe and sound, on two trips.

I receded into a corner, and tried to make myself as small and inconspicuous as possible. I stole a look at my watch. Just seconds to go now. I closed my eyes and—

***

That feeling never got old. I was smiling. That smell of beer -- I didn't even drink the stuff anymore -- but its smell was insistent, all around me, and told me before I opened my eyes a split second later that I was back in the past. Yeah, they liked their beer back here, and it had a more pungent smell than where and when I'd just been, and now the shirts and the jeans and the wide ties and moustaches and beads confirmed that I was in 1970 or some time pretty close to it. It was also sweltering in this car -- beer, sweat, and an overlay of primitive air conditioning. I felt as if I was inside a big malfunctioning refrigerator with its doors flung open—

"George?" A redhead approached, and ushered me to the door. "The passenger cars are a little cooler," she said.

"You work for Ian?" I asked, but I knew she did.

"Yes, I'm Ilana." She held the door open for me. We walked to the next car, which was definitely less oppressive. She leaned again a seat. "No point in sitting, you'll be getting off in Wilmington in just a few minutes."

I nodded, and noticed her tight blue bell-bottom jeans. Perfect attire for near the end of the psychedelic era.

She gave me a small stuffed envelope. "You've got a round-trip ticket, Wilmington to New York today, New York to Wilmington tomorrow, and another ticket from Wilmington back to New York. Plus $500 in time-current cash."

"Thanks," I said.

She regarded me. "You don't mind traveling down here to Wilmington just to go back to New York?"

"Small inconvenience for a miracle," I said.

"I like your attitude," she said and patted my arm. A toucher --

I liked that in a woman. "Be safe," she continued. "You chose the non-accompany option up to New York. I'll see you on the way back."

That was my cue to head for the doors.

"Wilmington. Wilmington, Delaware," the conductor announced on a too-loud speaker that hurt my ears.

***

I walked out of the train on to the Wilmington platform and looked for the stairs. I'm a big man, not as young as I used to be. I didn't mind the long walk down but didn't relish the prospect of the long walk back up to catch the northbound Metroliner to New York. I wasn't thrilled about the rickety elevator, either, but it was preferable to the stairs.

First I had to change into more 1970s-appropriate clothes. Given the anything-goes attitudes of this era, my garb hadn't attracted any undue attention on the Metroliner south of Philadelphia to here. But I didn't want to push my luck for the longer stay in New York, and I certainly didn't want to be wearing this vest on that northbound train, which could yank me right out of 1970 and back to the time I had just left. All of this in addition to my other reason for needing these new clothes.

I located the locker, exhaled with relief when the combination worked -- I'm always anxious about combination locks, too - and retrieved the little satchel. Off to the men's room. I was too focused on changing clothes to hold my nose at the ambiance. But I glanced at the cut of my jib in the corroded mirror and was satisfied.

Back to the locker, deposit my just-removed future clothes, and up to the northbound train. It was right on time, nineteen minutes later.

***

I often wondered if there were others like me, people who had spent so much time in two times that they felt they belonged to both. Ian's files were impregnable, distributed in incomprehensible pieces in so many systems around the world that only one person could put them together -- Ian, who carried the script for how to do that in his head. My visual surveillance of Ian's premises had given me plenty of images of Ian's customers. None jumped out at me as denizens of two times, and I certainly couldn't question them without risking Ian's anger and likely refusal to do any further business with me, i.e., take my money.

I took a long, slow breath as the Metroliner made its way beneath the Hudson on the last link in its journey to New York City. I couldn't help feeling pretty good to be back here. Maybe it was these 1970 duds I had on, but my skin felt as if it belonged in this time and place. I realized that I was shaking my head and frowning. Whom was I kidding? There was a far deeper reason that made me feel I belonged here -- I had been born in the 20th century, for chrissakes, and had lived here most of my life.

"New York City, Pennsylvania Station," the conductor announced. "Last stop."

***

I caught a cab on 8th Avenue. "Yorkvillle Restaurant, East 86th Street," I told the cabbie. "Know where that is?"

"No, you tell me when we get to 86," the cabbie replied in some sort of thick Slavic accent. If I'd put that in a movie, I'd be laughed out of the production. Truth could be funnier than fiction.

The Yorkville had one of the best cups of coffee in the city in this era. I looked forward to its fragrance and taste, but I wouldn't have time for more than one. I hoped my meeting with the go-ahead guy went quickly.

I directed the cabbie to the Yorkville, paid and tipped him and walked into the restaurant. Its dim lighting and smoky coolness were a welcome relief from the outside. I looked around and— Jeez, that Ian was full of surprises. Though I realized, as I often did, that nothing should surprise me about Ian.

I walked over to the table and extended my hand. "Elmyr de Hory ... no, no, please sit, no need to stand on my behalf."

Elmyr nodded. He looked tired, apprehensive about my speaking out his name, but appreciative that he didn't have to stand.

"How long have you been working for Ian?" I asked and sat at his table. "A coffee please," I said more loudly than Elmyr's name, and gestured to the waitress.

Elmyr waved my question away. "A once-in-a-while thing. Can't discuss," he spoke in a thick Hungarian accent. "Let's just say I like the money, and the protection, as you would know better than most."

"Ah yes, the forgeries."

Elmyr held a bony finger to his lips. "I'd like not to discuss that, either. My sole purpose now with you is to give the final green light on your project here."

"Understood," I said. The waitress arrived with my coffee. She looked older than my deceased grandmother. "It's a rather self-contained mission," I continued, "as you know."

Elmyr nodded. "But with its own dangers, anyway."

I lifted the coffee to my face. It smelled as good as ever. I sipped. The owner of the Yorkville likely had a relationship with some genius of a coffee supplier. I sipped some more, and looked at Elmyr. He'd been regarding me.

"You look good," he said. "The black outfit and the trimmed beard suit you."

I smiled. "Dressed for the part."

"But you did put on a few pounds," he added.

"Aways a battle," I replied.

Elmyr produced an envelope from his shabby jacket. "Ilana gave you the tickets and the money. This is your 1970 ID, in case you need it." He gave me the envelope. "Your counterpart's laid up with a sudden asthma attack, sleeping now under doctor's orders, and the phone connection is blocked. I assured him before the medication that his appearance was cancelled. You're all set."

"That easy?" I asked. "Not that I'm complaining."

"I'm not really comfortable talking to you in these circumstances," Elmyr said. "You know me too well." He managed an unhappy smile. "But we're two pros at this, you and I. No point in prolonging. You know what I'll say. 'Easy to slip in the asthma trigger in room service food.' I know what you'll say. 'Yeah, I'm a soft touch for anything to eat.' Any more questions?"

I shook my head no.

"Good, then, best luck." He cleared his throat, stood up, and shook my hand. He threw down a crumpled dollar for the coffee he'd been drinking.

I looked at my watch as Elmyr left the restaurant. Still time for another coffee and maybe a quick bite, actually. "Could you fill this up?" I called out to Methuselah's mother and held out my cup. "And a menu, too, please."

***

I caught a cab to the Elysee Theater on West 58th Street. I was a little early, I knew it, but Manhattan traffic was treacherous in any age and I couldn't risk being late. I was shown to the Green Room, offered a coffee -- which I refused, so as not to disrupt the taste of the Yorkville's brew, still on my tongue. But I accepted the proffered cigar. I was seated by a big, woefully fat TV screen. Another show -- not the Cavett -- was close to concluding. It was being taped, as would be mine for broadcast later in the evening. Always struck me as strange that an interview on a television show would be taped rather than broadcast live -- wasn't the big deal about television that it could be broadcast live, unlike a motion picture? -- but that was the least strange in what was about to happen, and I had worked so hard to set in motion.

I lit my cigar and puffed. I had memorized everything I had said the first time, like words in a play, because I simply couldn't fathom what, if anything, might ensue in the world if I said anything significantly different this time. The interview on the screen concluded. The talent girl shortly appeared in a mini-skirt that was just perfect and escorted me to the back of the studio. She whispered that I would go on stage as soon as Mr. Cavett finished his monologue. Her lips near my ear excited me, but I had to focus on what was just ahead.

Cavett introduced me in glowing terms. He described me as "unique". I suppressed a chortle. I heard Citizen Kane and War of the Worlds. He quoted Charlton Heston and Kenneth Tynan about me. "Will you welcome ... Orson Welles."

I walked out to a big round of sustained applause. I soaked it in, because I could never get enough. I shook Cavett's hand and couldn't help smiling. I bowed slightly to the audience. I didn't get appreciated like this in future. My own fault for disguising my real identity in that age -- to just about everyone except a few close friends and Ian -- and going with my first name, George.

The interview went just as I recalled, had seen, and rehearsed in the mirror at least a dozen times. I said goodbye to Cavett and left the studio. Part one of this business had concluded. I was looking forward to watching this on YouTube -- still what, more than a quarter century away? -- and seeing if I could notice slight differences in tone and delivery between this and my original interview on the Cavett show. There would be slight differences despite my best efforts, I knew that, even though the words were the same. I was my future self, not an exact copy of who I was now, after all. But that was actually the point of this.

***

I took a cab to my hotel on Madison Avenue -- a few blocks from where my counterpart was now sleeping it off at the Barclay Hotel -- and settled in for the evening. I couldn't resist rewarding myself with a little room service, but just of the culinary kind. It arrived quickly. I sipped and munched, and considered my next moves.

Part two of this operation was now commencing. I -- or a reasonable facsimile thereof -- had to be on that southbound Metroliner by tomorrow afternoon, to avoid arousing Ian's attention. This meant I had less than 24 hours to convince my younger self to take that excursion.

I fell asleep sooner than expected, awoke early the next morning, and had a fine breakfast of poached eggs and fresh figs. I headed over to the Barclay. I had no trouble getting a replacement for a "lost key" to my counterpart's room -- after all, I looked just like him, give or take a few pounds. It occurred to me that I wouldn't have to go through even this little pretense in my new adopted age -- Ian's age -- since my iris would have been all that I needed to enter my counterpart's room. He of course had the same iris. Well, I guess there were some things I could miss about that age.

As I left the elevator and approached his room, I played a minor fantasy in my head. If he had been in bed asleep with one of his/my women -- there were at least four possibilities, if memory served -- and I managed to remove him from the bed, take off my clothes, and snuggle right up to her, would she realize the difference when she awoke? Not likely, even if she sensed I weighed a tad more. She wouldn't let herself entertain the cognitive dissonance, to say the least, that being in bed with some other version of him -- me -- would cause her.

I entered my counterpart's room. He was in bed alone, alas, as I

knew he'd be. He awoke almost immediately. "What the hell?" He looked at me, rubbed his eyes and sat up too fast in bed. He grabbed the side of his back. I could feel his pain.

"You think you're dreaming," I said, as soothingly as possible. "You're not, but there's no way I can convince you of that right now. So you can just assume you're dreaming, let's talk, and eventually you'll know that you're not dreaming."

"You could spill cold water on my head, and if I don't wake up—"

"Nah, you know better than that -- wouldn't prove a thing, no more than Samuel Johnson's kicking the stone proved anything," I said. "The water and the stone could still be part of your or God's or who knows who else's dream."

He almost smiled, then recalled something unpleasant. "How'd I get here? I was -- wait -- the asthma attack! I was given a drug -- you're likely just a reaction to that, like Marley's ghost was the product of Scrooge's upset stomach-"

I laughed. "Marley's ghost was real in A Christmas Carol, not a figment of Scrooge's unsettled imagination."

My counterpart nodded slowly and looked confused.

"It's ok. Just keep thinking that you're dreaming me and this conversation now, as I said. The important thing is that we talk."

"I was supposed to be on the Cavett show last night," my counterpart said.

I took a seat, even though none had been offered. "Actually, you were -- or, in actual fact, I was."

"So ...," my counterpart began. "Mind you, I'm not accepting that you're anything more than a dream, though, at this point, who knows if you're a bad or a good one. But why—"

"I had your asthma attack induced, made sure you were drugged, and went on the Cavett show in your stead."

Now he laughed. "You -- I -- have a good imagination. I'll give you that. But why—"

I interrupted his same phrase again. I wanted to get to the point of this as soon as possible. "I wanted to establish me -- my version of you, with whatever subtle differences -- to the world back here as easily and quickly and graphically as possible. What better way than me not you appearing on Cavett?"

"And forgive me -- I'd rather not keep saying 'but why' again -- but the purpose of your wanting to establish yourself in my place back here was?"

I could tell he was enjoying this, at least a little. I doubted he'd enjoy what I was about to say to him. It would turn this presumed dream into a bit of a nightmare. "You're going to drop dead of a heart attack in 15 years -- in 1985. I won't -- I've already been treated for the condition and cured of it."

Right, now he wasn't smiling at all. "And where exactly would that be?"

"Not where, man, when. In the future, well after this century."

He shook his head, muttered something about needing some food to clear it, and went for the room service menu.

"Could you order the same for me?" I asked, softly. "You can afford the price of two breakfasts." I'd already eaten, but I had a much deserved reputation as a gourmand. And I didn't feel I was mooching -- I was pretty sure I'd wind up paying the bill, when I took control of his funds back here, and he did the same with some of mine in the future.

***

Our food arrived not long after. I opened the door, gestured to where the tray should be placed, and tipped the waiter.

"Thank you, Mr. Welles," he said, brightly. He glanced and nodded without really looking at my counterpart, who had put on a bathrobe. The waiter left the room.

I chuckled at the way he had avoided looking directly at my counterpart. Must have been his bathrobe. Better waiters and bellhops never looked long at anyone not fully clothed. "If you think she's naked, just look at her eyes, never a bit below, that's how we conduct ourselves in this profession," I had once heard a Brit dispense this advice.

My counterpart sat resignedly at the table. "He clearly saw you. I guess that's a point in favor of you being real," he said in that trademarked basso-profundo voice of ours.

"True, but not conclusive," I replied. "You still could be dreaming all of this, including the room service delivery."

He nodded, took a piece of his egg over easy, and smacked his lips. "So you come from the future, back to Mr. Dickens and his ghosts, or my almost namesake, Wells, Herbert George," he said.

"That's right," I said, and took a bit of the egg myself. Delicious.

"But the actual reality of time travel is far more complex than Dickens or even H. G. imagined."

"Of course," my counterpart said. "Reality is always crazier than fiction." He gestured to me. "Why don't you sketch out your whole story, as long as you're here in my dream or whatever. There could be a script in this, me thinks."

"I knew you'd warm up to this," I said. "Here's the nub of it: I'm a future version of you -- or, you, in the future. I've been cured of what will cause a massive, fatal heart attack in you, as I indicated. I came back here, and am talking to you now, with the goal of getting you to return to the future in my stead, so you can receive our life-saving treatment."

"But ... hasn't that already happened? I mean ... if you are here now, and you are my future self as you claim to be, doesn't that mean that I already went into the future, and received that treatment?"

"You're good," I said, and nodded in appreciation of my earlier self's quick grasp of some of the issue. "But, as I told you, time travel in reality -- at least insofar as I know it -- is far more complicated than what H. G. Wells wrote about in The Time Machine."

"Enlighten me."

I took the pot of coffee, and poured some for myself and my counterpart. "I remember my being you. I recall this very conversation, except I was sitting in your seat, and I don't know who the hell was sitting in mine -- well, I wasn't sure then, thought it was a dream, just as you do, now -- but now I, sipping this coffee and talking to you, of course do know it was me, back then, the future version of you that I am right now."

My counterpart shook his head slightly. "I'm thinking I may need something stronger than food and coffee. But yes, isn't what you just said tantamount to what I was just saying about this conversation -- and I assume everything after -- having already happened? But—"

"I don't really know how free will fits into this," I responded. "You believe you have control over your actions, right?"

"As much as any man," he chuckled and cleared his throat.

"Well, then, that's why I'm here to convince you to do this -- to travel into the future in my stead. Because, I'd rather not contemplate what would happen if you did not."

"Try me," he requested.

"I'd likely blink out of existence, the instant you decided not to travel to the future," I replied, "which would confirm your sense that this is a dream. Or maybe I never would have showed up this morning -- or last night, on Cavett -- at all."

He sipped his coffee, very slowly. "Given that there is a good chance that this is just a dream -- and one I'm now actually becoming quite fond of -- and, if not, well, it would be exciting, astonishing, to see what the future is like, I think I can say I'm game to do this." He thrust his hand across the table, for me to shake.

I shook it. "Good, I'm relieved."

"So, how would this work? I just step outside the door to this room and into your future?"

"Not quite so simple," I replied.

***

We spent the rest of the morning and a good part of the afternoon discussing what was not quite so simple. Most of it was the plethora of detail he had to know about my future life in order to pass for me. And then there was Ian.

"He thinks it will be me returning to the future, not you," I said.

"You told me you paid a small fortune for this trip," my younger self replied. "Why the hell should he care?"

"Trust me, he cares," I replied. "I paid for a trip to sit in for you on Dick Cavett -- I knew he wouldn't be likely to object to that. But that's a far cry, a universe of difference, from you returning to the future instead of me."

"So raise more funds and pay the man for the different mission."

I shook my head no. "Ian is not just about money, though he likes to give the impression that it's all he cares about. But he also has an abiding concern, an unclear but I suspect absolute list of do's and don't's, about what he allows his customers to do on their trips to the past."

"Who is this guy?"

"I've studied him. I've learned a lot, but he's still a cypher."

My counterpart shook his head and scoffed, slightly. "We're the same person -- more alike than identical twins. Ian obviously knows you traveled to the past. He'll assume it's you who's returned. If he notices any difference in our affect, in my mien versus yours, he'd attribute that to the impact of this very trip on you, wouldn't he?"

"I suppose," I said. "Look, I'm not trying to talk you out of this -- last thing I would do -- I just want you to be as aware as possible of what you'll be up against when you give the vest back to Ian."

***

We swapped wallets, clothes, and I made sure my counterpart had my ticket for the 4:25pm southbound Metroliner from Penn Station. I continued to brief him, and we left in time to catch the train.

Leaving the hotel separately would have been a little less likely to attract attention, but I figured the greater risk still resided in his bolting when he left my sight, so we walked out of the hotel together. I hailed a taxi -- less exposure than taking the subway, and less than walking from here to Penn Station, would which have been too tiring for us, anyway, especially in this torrid heat. We might even get an air-conditioned cab -- there were some of them already in service in 1970 -- and if not we'd roll down the windows, and cool down the good old-fashioned way.

"You know, I met H. G. once, in a radio interview in Texas in 1940," my younger self mused, as our taxi slowly made its way with wide-open windows down Seventh Avenue.

"I know, I remember," I replied, and indeed recalled that with pleasure.

"Amazing man," my counterpart continued. "He even plugged Citizen Kane in that interview. After he thanked me for sparking more sales of War of the Worlds."

I nodded.

"Seems like a dream, another lifetime," he continued. "Was I dreaming that, too?"

"You're not dreaming this and you weren't dreaming that," I said.

"And the insane thing is, I think I almost believe you," he said.

I squeezed his shoulder. "I'm glad. You should."

"His name is George, too, as you know," my counterpart mused. "Herbert George Wells. So in addition to having the same last name except for one letter, we both share a same given name -- George Orson Welles, Herbert George Wells .... Was he somehow us, too??"

I chuckled. "Not likely," I said. "His voice was much higher, and he had a great British accent."

"I suppose anything is possible in a dream, though," my counterpart said.

***

I realized that our cab hadn't moved much in the past few minutes. We were on 38th Street and Seventh Avenue -- just a few minutes away from Penn Station -- but only, of course, if our taxi was moving. I looked at my watch.

My counterpart saw that, and did the same with his. "We have 35 minutes to get to the station. Shouldn't be a problem, assuming —"

"Yeah." I hadn't wanted to get to the station too early -- so as not to attract attention as big twins, especially not Ilana's attention, if she happened to be somewhere in the waiting room. But missing the train was unacceptable.

Our cabbie honked his horn. Didn't do any good. I stuck my head out the window, craned my neck, and saw the problem: an overheated car about half way down the block, hood in the air, steaming like a hot dog stand. Traffic was frozen in the heat. Our cabbie honked again and turned his head around to us. "Sorry," he said. "Bad time of day."

I pulled out my wallet and paid him. "Keep the change."

My younger self and I got out of the taxi. "We'll have to walk it," I told him.

"Obviously," he said, grunted, and wiped his brow.

It was hotter outside than in the cab. Fortunately, we both were dressed for it. But I had to be careful not to make my counterpart walk too fast, given his health. If he dropped dead right here in the street, so would I – or disappear, at any rate.

I continued to go over details with him. We stopped for a few beats at every corner, so he could catch his breath. I appreciated the breaks, too.

We reached the station, with 16 minutes to spare. We were both sweating profusely. "You can wash up in the bathroom on the train," I told my counterpart. "They're not too bad in this era."

"I know," he said.

"Right." I described Ilana again. "You'll enjoy looking at her body."

That got a smile from him.

"Make sure you see a doctor as soon as you get home -- to my home," I said. "You'll find listings on any screen. Get that heart taken care of, first order of business. There may be other things you'll need to do, later on -- other trips through time. All in due course. I don't want to overload you now."

"Considerate of you," he half growled, laughed, then coughed— and suddenly grabbed his chest and winced in pain—

God no! I started to react—

He doubled over in pain.

I put my arms around him and tried to hold him up—

He broke free, staggered— and laughed heartily. "Sorry -- only joking!"

Good, he was ok. "Thanks -- that almost gave me a heart attack." I mock punched him in the arm, and kept an eye on him as he walked towards his train. I turned and went back out into the heat. A fine little piece of acting on his part. But of more interest to me now was that apparently the past could be changed, at least slightly. I was 99% sure I had not feigned that heart attack the first time around.

***

I took a taxi back to what was now my hotel room -- unlike the taxi, blessedly air conditioned. I stretched out on the bed. The maid had tidied the room. I'd have to remember to give her a big tip. I wondered how long it would take before I got any indication that my younger self had made it back to the future ok. I didn't have to wait long. The phone in the room rang.

"Mr. Welles?" the receptionist at the front desk asked me. "A man by the name of 'Elmer' here to see you, with a friend."

I thought for a quick second. I supposed I could run from this now, but I was tired, and, besides, sooner or later I'd have to face it. "Thank you -- please send them up."

They knocked on my door a few minutes later.

I opened it with a smile.

There stood Elmyr de Hory and the friend -- Ian.

***

I invited them in. Elmyr cracked a craggy grin. Ian looked just as he had every time I'd seen him -- a scowl etched on his face. But it was little disconcerting seeing him out of his element, away from his shop with the neon sign.

"So you recovered all right from the asthma?" Elymyr asked, now straight-faced.

For a split second, I thought maybe Elmyr -- and therefore Ian -- thought I was my younger self, whom Elmyr had inflicted with asthma yesterday, and I had just brought to Penn Station less than an hour ago. No, these guys were way too smart for that.

Elmyr smiled again. "Had you going for a minute there, didn't I? It was good seeing you at the Yorkville last night," he said, just so I'd know for sure that he knew for sure just who I was.

"Same here." Everyone was the comedian today. I gestured to a small table. The three of us pulled up chairs.

I looked at Ian, and recalled an old theater adage. There were some actors who found the spotlight, wherever they happened to be on stage. They stole the scene, were stars, whatever the script and the director might have intended. Ian, sitting here, had that talent.

He spoke right up. "You're in gross violation of the itinerary," he said to me.

"What can I do to compensate you?" I replied, knowing better than to deny his allegation.

"The pertinent clause says that if you don't return, I'm entitled to seize all of your assets."

I considered. "Someone with my DNA, my memories, even the nasal suppositories you left in my vest pocket, did return."

"True," Ian said. "But not all of your memories. Not you."

"True," I replied. "But you'd have a hard time proving that."

"He's younger than you," Ian said.

"Precise age isn't so easy to scientifically ascertain -- the world wears our bodies in different ways."

Ian nodded his acknowledgement of the point.

"And would you really want to make a Federal -- or whatever it would be -- case of this?" I pressed my advantage.

"No, but given your considerable assets in my time, I would risk it," Ian said. "I could petition to have all the legal proceedings private, sealed from the public. I have friends in good places."

I had likely reached the limits of my argument.

Ian saw that I realized that.

"May I ask how you found out? And when?" I knew Ian could have realized the switch any time in the future, and, whenever that was, set his visit to today.

"He told me," Ian answered, matter-of-factly.

"He? You mean ... my younger self?"

"That's right, and he told me right away." Now I got that slight smile from Ian, worse than his scowl.

"Did he at least get his heart fixed?"

"Your heart's fine, isn't it?" Ian said. "I sent him straight to the doctor, as soon he told me your story."

I touched my chest, breathed in and out, and considered. "So take all of my damned money in the future -- that'll bankrupt him, not me." And I had squirreled away a sizeable portion of my funds in the future, for whenever I returned. It was likely beyond Ian's and definitely my younger self's reach .... But was Ian telling me the truth about my younger self? I certainly had no recollection of having had such a conversation with Ian as my younger self. But he probably had panicked for some reason, this time around, when he finally became convinced that what was happening to him wasn't a dream, but—

"There may be another way," Ian said, "something you could do for me that would balance the books."

Here it came. As I had told my younger self, Ian had goals that went way beyond the money he always claimed he was all about .

***

I had breakfast in the Barclay the next morning -- eggs over easy, English muffin, fresh figs, and orange juice, fresh squeezed. I had to admit -- eggs didn't taste quite as good in the future.

My waiter, Lenny, was talkative. "Saw you on Cavett the other night -- you were excellent. Can I offer a little casting advice?"

"Sure." I'd likely get it whether I agreed or not.

"You ought to cast Brando in your next movie -- Brando! -- he's still the best. And Bronson as supporting actor. You see the body on that guy? I wish I could be in such good shape."

"Tell me about it," I said, only a little less tartly than the orange juice.

Lenny laughed. "Hey, you're entitled. You're the director, for godsakes. Doesn't matter what you look like."

"I used to act. Still do, sometimes."

"Point taken," Lenny said, and clapped me on the back. "But can I give you a little more advice -- in your capacity as director?"

"Sure."

"George Pal did a fine job with War of the Worlds and Time Machine -- I actually liked his Destination Moon and When Worlds Collide better -- but you could a better job, really, with any H. G. Wells story."

I nodded. "Thank you."

"He sometimes stays here when he's in from Hollywood," Lenny said, quietly, conspiratorially. "Wouldn't say he's a pal of mine, but almost." Lenny laughed at his own pun. "Don't tell Mr. Pal I said anything about his movies. But I'm telling ya, you're the director as far as H. G. Wells goes."

***

I don't know if anyone else has ever had this experience, but I sometimes almost think that waiters are reading my mind -- and not about food -- when they recognize me and give me advice.

I left a generous tip on my room tab, patted off whatever may have been left of the egg on my face -- visible and otherwise, for the many failures and unfulfilled projects in my life. Well, this was one project I could not afford to leave hanging. I left the cafe and allowed the guy in front of the hotel to call over a cab for me. "Penn Station," I told the cabbie. Felt like that's all I had been saying to cabbies these days. But the deja vu went a lot deeper than that.

The cab got to the station in plenty of time. I looked at the board and noted the track for my train -- to Wilmington. But I knew I wouldn't be seeing Ilana again on this train. I half-consciously touched my chest. No need for the specially woven vest, either. It wouldn't be waiting for me in the locker in Wilmington Station. My counterpart had already taken it, yesterday. And I had no need for it. I wouldn't be traveling through time, this time.

I boarded the train, and tried to make myself comfortable in my seat. But there would be not much comfort in this trip, not in my seat or my skin, and not much enjoyment in the clothes and colors and culture of 1970, either. That probably came from my discomfort at being a guinea pig, a pawn, of Ian's, rather than his client. But what did it matter? It's not as if his clients had much control over their destinies, either. And what choice did I have? Ian had a monopoly on the time travel which had become the lifeblood of my life, because I had made it that way.

I fidgeted when the train pulled into Philadelphia. This is where I had left my seat the other day on the way to the Cafe Car and its exit to the past. No need for the Cafe Car today. I was already in the past.

The train pulled out of Philadelphia and soon was in Wilmington. I left the train and caught a taxi. "Telegraph office," I instructed, and provided the address.

***

"It's an experimental process," Ian had explained to me, back in the hotel room. "My team has been working on it for years. The possibilities are profound, as you'll no doubt agree."

I had never seen Ian so ... eager ... so much the pitchman. But I agreed with his assessment. People could travel as far back as 1969 on the Tricela-Metroliner route. If this telegraph gambit worked, Ian's clients could eventually send telegrams from a few years before 2006 -- when the last words-only telegram was sent out for hand delivery by Western Union -- to as far back in time as 1848, when the central telegraph office started doing business in Wilmington, Delaware on Front and King Streets.

I tipped the cabbie copiously, and entered the Western Union office. There were two tellers, each with a line of customers. I got at the end of the shorter line and waited. Each of the three people in front of me sent money orders. The teller counted the bills in slow, exaggerated motions.

I finally stepped up to the teller. He had white hair and a ruddy face, and was likely in his early 60s. "I have an old-fashioned kind of telegram to send," I said, and laughed. "Just words, no money."

"Yes, sir."

I gave him a sheet of paper, on which the message I wished to send was carefully, and I hope clearly, printed.

"Can I read this to you, sir?" he inquired.

"Yes, please do," I replied.

The teller began. "Mr. Herbert George Wells, 123 Eardley Road, Sevenoaks, Kent, England," he read aloud. "Is that right for the name and address?"

"Yes." I could tell from his tone and demeanor -- unless he was a world-class actor -- that he'd never heard the name. Likely because the recipient of the telegram was better known by his first two initials, or maybe this teller was no fan of science fiction, who knew. But in any case it was a good thing, because it saved me the trouble of explaining why I was sending a telegram in 1970 to a man who had died in 1946.

The teller cleared his throat. I realized I had been staring at him. "And please read the message now," I said.

He complied. "Strongly urge you to bring Chronic Argonauts"

-- he stumbled slightly over the last word, but pronounced it tolerably well - "into full bloom as a novel STOP Will sell well STOP Will inspire you to write other novels STOP Indeed a device just aborning called the wireless telegraph as per Tesla and Lodge will later help greatly with sales of those novels STOP You will thank me for this many years later when we speak together through this wireless for an interview"—

I nodded that that was the message. I enjoyed hearing the word STOP -- Ian, ever the penny pincher, would likely have instructed me to use it instead of the period in any case, since punctuation was charged for, but STOP was a Western Union freebie. But that was not the reason he had included it in this message, every word of which he had dictated to me, without even going through the motions of making sure I agreed that the content worked with what I knew of H. G. Wells. Fortunately, I thought that it did.

"Ok," the teller said. "And you would like this signed, 'An American admirer with a similar name'."

"Yes."

"That's a little long for a signature," the teller said.

"That's the way I want it," I replied. "You can charge me for it," I added, helpfully.

"You pay for every word, Sir, except the STOP used in lieu of the period."

Charming. But no wonder the telegram had gone the way of hieroglyphics.

***

I stepped out of the office into the street and the heat. The late afternoon sun was even worse than in New York. Not surprising -- I was, after all, further south.

But Ian was perpetually surprising. What he hoped to accomplish with this telegraph connection to the past, and how he thought it would work, had truly floored me.

"You can't change so much as a letter in the telegram," he had instructed me. "No ad libbing, as you might be tempted to do in your craft of acting."

So he's a critic, too, I had thought. But I had permitted myself a question. "Why?"

Ian had looked at me for a few moments, as if sizing me up as to whether I could understand what he was about to tell me. He apparently concluded that I could. "It's not the precise sense of the words that I most care about. It's the electronic signal that their commission to the telegraph will produce."

"I'm not sure I understand." Though I thought I had an inkling of where he was going with this.

Ian obliged me. "The Morse Code, in addition to its translatabilty into these words -- based, of course, on the arbitrary assignment of electronic signals to letters -- will also have an effect that is not arbitrary at all. That signal, and only that specific, exact signal, will both connect into the temporal anomaly north of Wilmington, the one that made your travel to here possible—"

"Right," I said.

"—that signal, and only that specific, exact signal," he repeated, with a glare for my interruption, "will not only be sent across the sea to England -- as any telegram could be sent today in 1970 -- but, because of its entwinement with the Wilmington anomaly, will ignite its sending to England in 1894."

"Was there even transatlantic cable in 1894?" I asked.

"It was laid down right after the U.S. Civil War. A major engineering feat of its day."

"So the specific signal is the equivalent of the vest," I had mused.

"The precise Morse code signal is the equivalent of the weave."

"Yes."

"To move not people but information back in time," I said.

"Yes."

"Information back in time to H. G. Wells," I said.

"Yes," Ian replied, now monosyllabic.

I took it in, as best I could. "But ... why?"

***

I had known the answer to that would require a lot more than one word. How much Ian chose to tell me, of course, was another matter ...

I stopped my reverie and looked around for a cab. Would it be air conditioned? Yes! Lucky break at last, and a hell of a lot better than this wilting Wilmington heat.

"Wilmington Station," I told the driver.

"I have quite a lucrative business," Ian had replied to my question, back in my hotel room, "as you no doubt have gathered. H. G. Wells's Time Machine, though pretty far in the past, was a necessary start-up factor."

"Because it got the world thinking about time travel?"

"That's right," Ian had replied. "Oh, there were a few stories before, but The Time Machine really put time travel on the intellectual map. Without any intervention from me, Wells would likely have expanded "The Chronic Argonauts" story into *The Time Machine* novel anyway -- his biographers say he was hungry for a larger audience -- but I'm thinking a little extra nudge can't hurt, a little insurance that history does the right thing for me."

I had looked at Ian. Behind his meticulous, scowling confidence was a bit more insecurity than I would have expected.

And he had smiled back at me, genuinely, for an instant. "Yes, there's no such thing as too much of a good thing when it comes to making sure history is on your side."

***

My cab arrived at the Wilmington station. I paid the cabbie and took the shaky elevator up to the northbound platform. God, it seemed as it was more than two lifetimes ago when I had been in this dingy, odiferous box. But that was, what, just two days ago?

I had had one last question of Ian, back at the Barclay in New York just yesterday.

"Why me?" I had asked Ian. "Why do you need me to send the telegram to H. G. Wells?"

"I've done this myself -- used that office in Wilmington to send telegrams to the past -- and the process worked fine. But you have some sort of cosmic entwinement with H. G. Wells -- the closeness of your names, your intersection with him in the early part of your career, convinced me that you were the ideal person to send this extraordinary telegram. For all I've been able to do with time travel, I still think of it as a toddler that needs all the support it can get.

"Bring Western Union -- Western Un-ion -- into Ian's Ions and Eons," I mused, and pronounced the second word as "un" and "ion" to make my point.

"That's right," Ian had said, "though I prefer the French pronunciation of 'un' - meaning 'one,' or one with the ions."

***

My train arrived. I had to remind myself again that I wouldn't be time traveling on this one -- it was 1970 now, and it would be 1970 when I reached New York.

But I had sent information back in time, to H. G. Wells, in 1894. I took a seat by the window, and looked out, as my train slid out of the station. Yeah, it had apparently worked with me -- Ian had gotten what we wanted. After all, I was here on this train in 1970, I had come back here from the future, after booking my trip in Ian's Ions and Eons, and my heart felt fine.

But the impact of this message to the past had been only to buttress what my almost namesake Herbert George Wells had already been on his way to doing, anyway. And as I looked out at the rapidly receding shrubs and rust of the Wilmington train station, I had to wonder: now that I had helped Ian validate this process, what would happen when he sold people the means of sending messages to the past intended not to support but change or undo history? Would Ian do that?

"Excuse me -- are you Orson Welles?" a leggy brunette, with a high, stylish, mauve mini-skirt or some such asked me.

"Yes," I replied, not very warmly. If I hadn't been so engrossed in thinking about Ian, I might have invited her to sit down next to me.

She started to turn—

"Care to join me?" I asked her, in the most inviting baritone I could muster. I gestured to the empty seat next to me.

Her eyes lit up. "Yes, thank you!" She sat down. "I saw you on the Dick Cavett Show night before last -- you were very clever, Mr. Welles."

"Call me George," I said. "It comes before the Orson."

She smiled. "I'm Isabella."

ABOUT THE AUTHOR

Paul Levinson

 Paul Levinson, PhD, is Professor at Fordham University. His science fiction novels include The Silk Code (winner of the Locus Award for Best First Science Fiction Novel of 1999), The Consciousness Plague, The Pixel Eye, Borrowed Tides, The Plot to Save Socrates, Unburning Alexandria, Chronica, and It's Reall Life: An Alternate History of The Beatles . His novelette "The Chronology Protection Case" was made into a short film and is on Amazon Prime Video. His alternate history short story about The Beatles, "It's Real Life," was made into a radio play, was a finalist for the Sidewise Award for Alternate History, and was expanded into a novel in 2024 . His novelette, "Robinson Calculator," was published in the Robots Through the Ages anthology in July 2023. He was President of the Science Fiction Writers of America (SFWA) 1998-2001. His nonfiction books, including The Soft Edge, Digital McLuhan, Cellphone, Realspace, and New New Media, have been translated into 15 languages. He has appeared on CBS, CNN, MSNBC, the History Channel, and NPR. His 1972 album, Twice Upon A Rhyme, was re-issued in Japan and Korea in 2008, and in the U. K. in 2010. His first new album since 1972, Welcome Up: Songs of Space and Time, was released by Old Bear Records and Light in the Attic Records in 2020.

BOOKS BY THIS AUTHOR

It's Real Life: An Alternate History Of The Beatles

It's 1996, and in this alternate history novel about the Beatles, WFUV disc jockey Pete Fornatale walks in the tunnels under Fordham University, then travels downtown to Grand Central Terminal and finds the world of music that he inhabits is very different. As he struggles to understand how to get in and out of alternate realities, and make sure John Lennon is not killed in any of them, Fornatale will actually dine with John Lennon and David Bowie, consult with Leonard Cohen, attend a Beatles concert with Diana Ross in Central Park in 1996, and work with a variety of real life characters you may or may not have heard of. The short story this novel is based upon won the Mary Shelley Award for Outstanding Fiction in 2023, and was a Finalist for the Sidewise Award (short form) for Alternate History 2022.

The Plot To Save Socrates

Paul Levinson's astonishing science fiction novel is a surprise and a delight: In the year 2042, Sierra, a young graduate student in Classics, is shown a new dialog of Socrates, recently discovered, in which a time traveler tries to argue that Socrates might escape death by travel to the future! Thomas, the elderly scholar who has shown her the document, disappears, and Sierra immediately begins to track down the provenance of the manuscript with the help of her classical scholar boyfriend, Max.

The trail leads her to time machines in gentlemen's clubs in

London and in New York, and into the past--and to a time traveler from the future, posing as Heron of Alexandria in 150 AD. Complications, mysteries, travels, and time loops proliferate as Sierra tries to discern who is planning to save the greatest philosopher in human history. Fascinating historical characters from Alcibiades to William Henry Appleton, the great nineteenth-century American publisher, to Hypatia and Socrates himself appear. With surprises in every chapter, Paul Levinson has outdone himself in The Plot to Save Socrates.

Unburning Alexandria

Mid-twenty-first century time traveler Sierra Waters, fresh from her mission to save Socrates from the hemlock, is determined to alter history yet again, by saving the ancient Library of Alexandria - where as many as 750,000 one-of-a-kind texts were lost, an event described by many as "one of the greatest intellectual catastrophes in history."

Along the way she will encounter old friends such as William Henry Appleton the great 19th century American publisher and enemies like the enigmatic time travelling inventor Heron of Alexandria. And her quest will involve such other real historic personages as Hypatia, Cleopatra's sister Arsinoe, Ptolemy the astronomer, and St. Augustine - again placing her friends, her loved-ones, and herself in deadly jeopardy.

In this sequel to THE PLOT TO SAVE SOCRATES, award winning author Paul Levinson offers another time-traveling adventure spanning millennia, full of surprising twists and turns, all the while attempting the seemingly impossible: UNBURNING ALEXANDRIA.

Chronica

Sierra and Max arrive in 2062, and find the world has somewhat changed. Joe Biden was President from 2009-2017, and train travel is much more prominent. Was this due to the scrolls that she rescued from the Library of Alexandria? Heron's Chronica, which describes how to build a time travel device and was one of the texts Sierra saved from burning, has not yet been published, and Sierra soon realizes that Heron is doing everything in his lethal power to prevent that from happening. Her attempt to safeguard the Chronica, which she left in William Henry Appleton's keeping, takes her to the end of the 1890s, where she dines, plots, and otherwise interacts with John Jacob Astor IV, Nikola Tesla, Thomas Edison, J. P. Morgan, film pioneers William Dickson and Edwin Porter, and other denizens of The Gilded Age.

The Chronology Protection Case

When NYPD forensic detective Phil D'Amato takes a call from a lady physicist about her missing husband, he has no idea that her life, his life, and every other scientist working on a top-secret time travel project will soon be in dire jeopardy. As the number of dead begins to mount, D'Amato starts to realize that the suspect is not any one person or group but something much more sinister and dangerous. "The Chronology Protection Case" was a finalist for the Nebula Award for Best Science Fiction Novelette of 1995. The story was adapted into a low-budget movie by Jay Kensinger (now on Amazon Prime Video), and an Edgar-nominated radio play by Mark Shanahan.

The Copyright Notice Case

Can a code embedded in our DNA millennia ago kill people who violate the warning in the code? NYPD forensic detective Dr. Phil D'Amato investigates. His main source of information: a researcher with two X chromosomes and green-violet eyes.

The Silk Code

Phil D'Amato, an NYC forensic detective (also featured in several of Levinson's popular short stories and two subsequent novels), is caught in an ongoing struggle that dates all the way back to the dawn of humanity on Earth--and one of his best friends is a recent casualty. Unless Phil can unravel the genetic puzzle of the Silk Code, he'll soon be just as dead.

Winner Locus Award for Best First Science Fiction novel of 1999.

The Consciousness Plague

Dr. Phil D' Amato returns from The Silk Code, winner of the Locus Award for Best First Science Fiction Novel of 1999, with another blend of biological science fiction and hard-boiled police-procedural mystery.

Memory itself is the suspect in The Consciousness Plague - more particularly, loss of memory, in slivers of time deducted from a growing number of individuals, which plays havoc with everything from the investigation of serial stranglings to candlelight dinners. D'Amato, NYPD forensic detective, investigates a spate of unusual cases and finds evidence of a bacteria-like organism that has lived in our brains since our origin as a species and may be responsible for our very consciousness.

A new antibiotic crosses the blood-brain barrier and inadvertently kills this essential bug. Phil himself falls victim to this memory hole, and must struggle to get the proper authorities to pay attention before everyone loses so much memory that they forget that they forgot in the first place.

Winner of the 2003 Mary Shelley Award for Outstanding Fictional Work

The Pixel Eye

Squirrels are spying on us in the park. Mice may have organic bombs set to go off in their brains. Holograms are taking the place of real people. Phil D'Amato investigates a case that pits civil liberties versus national security as he seeks to ward off a major terrorist attack on near-future New York City.

Nominee for the Prometheus Award for Best Libertarian SF Novel

The Loose Ends Saga

Jeff Harris goes back in time to prevent the explosion of the space shuttle Challenger, but gets pulled into November 1963, and has 23 years to plan his intervention with the Challenger. He discovers that his actions in the past may result in the Soviet Union continuing in the 21st century. He strives with Laura and Karina to prevent this, and also the murder of John Lennon and the September 11 attacks, but the resilience and interconnections of history make it unlikely that they'll be able to stop all of those calamities, and the personal survival of at least one of them may be incompatible with their goals. The Saga contains Loose Ends -- the novella nominated for Hugo, Nebula, and Sturgeon Awards -- and its sequels Little Differences, Late Lessons, and Last Calls.

Ian's Ions And Eons

Ian's Ions and Eons is the name of a time-travel agency in the Riverdale neighborhood of the Bronx. This anthology contains the three "Ian" novelettes published thus far: "Ian's Ions and Eons" (2011) "Ian, Isaac, and John" (2011) and "Ian, George, and George" (2013). The time travel stories involve Presidential elections, rock music, television and movies. Real historical personages who appear include Al Gore, George W. Bush, William Rehnquist, David Bowie, John Lennon, Dick Cavett, and Orson Welles.

The Other Car

James Oleson is beginning to see everything in perfect duplicate - two identical models of cars which are the same down to scuff marks and license plate, two old philosophy books with the same torn pages and inscription in old ink, and twin mail men. Is he losing his mind, or experiencing the birth of a new alternate reality via binary fission?

Slipping Time

Tripping in the rain can be very helpful.

In The Dybuuk's Pocket

Beware whom you take presents from ....

Borrowed Tides

August 2016 brought news - real news, in our reality - that an Earth-like planet was discovered circling Proxima Centauri, the third star in the Alpha Centauri system, just over four light years from Earth. This is exactly what happens in Borrowed Tides, first published in hardcover in 2001, re-issued in Kindle this past April. It tells the story of the first starship to the Alpha Centauri system in 2029, employing a new technology which can move it through deep space at almost half the speed of light. But it requires an enormous amount of fuel, and can only carry enough for a one-way trip. A philosopher of science and his childhood friend, an anthropologist with a specialty in Native American culture, have a daringly bizarre plan, and talk the government into putting them in charge of the Light Through starship voyage.

Marilyn And Monet

It all started in the hot summer of 1960, when Marilyn Monroe walked off the set of The Misfits and began to hear a haunting song in her head, "Goodbye Norma Jean" ...

The Orchard

In the 22nd century, humans have discovered numerous planets teeming with life, but none with human-level intelligence. Teams of exo-biologists have been dispatched to the most promising places. The fifth planet of the Beta Hydri system has patches of trees that bear delicious fruit. Will it kill the exo-biologists before they can prove the planet has deliberately planted orchards - a sure sign of intelligent life - and get the news back to Earth?

The Orchard was a finalist for the 1998 Sturgeon Award for Best Short Science Fiction.

The Suspended Fourth

Have birds on the second planet of Delta Pavonis been bred to sing songs that warn the inhabitants of deadly danger?

Robinson Calculator

The Calculators -- a secretive group of androids -- have been living off the radar for centuries or longer. Why are they now burying their dead in plain view?

Urban Corridoes

an anthology of urban fantasy and science fiction stories, ranging from alternate realities to time travel to ghosts and androids and other strange things in the city